MICHELLE VERNAL LOVES a happy ending. She lives with her husband and their two boys in the beautiful and resilient city of Christchurch, New Zealand. She's partial to a glass of wine, loves a cheese scone, and has recently taken up yoga—a sight to behold indeed. As well as the Guesthouse on the Green series Michelle's written seven novels—they're all written with humour and warmth and she hopes you enjoy reading them. If you enjoy A Wedding at O'Mara's then taking the time to say so by leaving a review would be wonderful. A book review is the best present you can give an author. If you'd like to hear about Michelle's new releases, you can subscribe to her Newsletter via her website: www.michellevernalbooks.com.

To say thank you, you'll receive an exclusive O'Mara women character profile!

Also by Michelle Vernal

The Cooking School on the Bay
Second-hand Jane
Staying at Eleni's
The Traveller's Daughter
Sweet Home Summer
The Promise
When We Say Goodbye
And...
Introducing: The Guesthouse on the Green Series
Book 1 - O'Mara's
Book 2 – Moira-Lisa Smile
Book 3 – What Goes on Tour
Book 4 – Rosi's Regrets
Book 5 – Christmas at O'Mara's
A short story – New Year's Eve with the O'Maras
Book 6 – A Wedding at O'Mara's
And coming soon...
Book 7 – Maureen's Song

A Wedding at O'Mara's

by

Michelle Vernal

Chapter 1
Dublin 2000

Aisling O'Mara was feeling very grown up as she tottered down Baggot Street all tucked up inside her coat. She didn't have time to tap the young man on the shoulder who she'd spied spitting on the ground as he waited for the bus. She'd have liked to have told him spitting was a disgusting habit but had she done so, she knew she'd then fret she was morphing into her mammy. Nor did she have time to wonder why on earth that woman with the lank, greasy hair and a cigarette in one hand, a child clutching the other hadn't seen fit to put a hat on her little one. It was a day that clearly called for a hat. Never mind either the fact she was a woman in her mid-thirties about to be married at long last because Aisling was about to do the most grown up thing of her life. She was off to meet her soon-to-be husband and they had an appointment at the AIB Bank where they were going to open a joint account. It was very exciting!

Moira had called her a sad arse that morning over her enormous plate of toast which had been smothered in thick, sweet Magiun, plum jam. The jar had come courtesy of the guest-house's weekend breakfast cook, Mrs Baiku who hailed from Romania and Aisling was extremely partial to it. Mind you she was partial to most things with copious amounts of sugar in them. Life, she often lamented would have been a lot easier if her secret fantasy wasn't to roll in a ball pit filled with coconutty, marshmallow Snowballs. At that point in time too, finding herself staring at her paltry boiled egg with NO soldiers to dip because she was frantically trying to lose a few pounds before her big day, it had taken all her strength not to try and divert her sister from her breakfast.

Diversion tactics had worked a treat when they were younger and had saved her from many a serve of the broad bean or pile of spinach. It was simple, she'd turn to Moira, being the youngest and most gullible of her siblings and exclaim, 'How did that cat get in here?' Moira's head never failed to spin searching for a non-existent cat while Aisling would dump whatever was causing her angst on her plate onto her sister's. It worked the other way too when it came to snaffling an extra fish finger or the like. She never felt a smidgen of guilt either when she was allowed to leave the table thanks to her clean plate while Moira sat staring mournfully at a mound of something green and, by that time, stone cold while Mammy prattled on about how the starving children in Africa would be grateful for a good meal like Moira's to be placed in front of them and how she ought to be grateful. Aisling would think it served her right for always helping herself to her stuff. She'd tried the diversion tactics on Patrick once, given Mammy always gave him an extra fish finger because he was the boy, but he'd caught her out and smacked her hard on her knuckles with his fork.

This morning at the breakfast table, however, Aisling had drawn on her inner willpower, of which there wasn't much, but what little there was had been enough for her to leave Moira's toast alone. She'd been tempted to pick it up and flick her in the face with it though as she sneered across the table at the fact her elder sister was about to share her finances wholeheartedly with her fiancé.

'A joint account? What's mine is yours and what's yours is mine. Feck that, what's mine is mine thanks very much,' she'd stated.

Given that Moira, a self-proclaimed poor art student these days, didn't have anything other than a collection of pricey cosmetics and some expensive and very impractical items of clothing in her wardrobe, Aisling had rolled her eyes, cracked the shell on her boiled egg and told her sister in a suitably condescending manner that one day if say Tom, for instance, was to pop the question then she'd understand.

Now, spying Quinn up ahead, waiting as he'd promised he would be, with his hands shoved in the pockets of his jacket as he stamped his feet against the cold, she grinned at him waving out. He spotted her through the bobbing heads of people ducking and diving along pavements not designed to cope with the influx their city had seen this last couple of years and strode towards her. She was pleased to note he'd listened to her and dressed in his good jeans – his going out jeans – not that they went out much. There wasn't much time for that between him running Quinn's, his busy bistro, and her managing the guesthouse with its unpredictable hours. He'd laughed when she'd told him he needed to look smart and presentable to meet Mr Cleary.

'Aisling, the days of going cap in hand to see the bank manager are long gone. Sure, they're desperate for our business,' he'd said. Quinn had plans of them putting a down payment on a house. Not for them to live in – he was going to move into

O'Mara's with her and Moira after they were married – but as a rental property. 'Property prices are high, but rental property is in high demand. It's as good a time as any for us to get our feet on the property ladder,' he'd said. He'd gone so far as to get the calculator out and bang out figures based on his and her savings and had been confident that after the wedding, 'and the honeymoon,' she'd added, they could start looking around to get an idea of what was on the market.

His nose was red from the chill air, Aisling saw as he drew nearer. The reason he'd been standing about outside his restaurant instead of waiting inside in the toasty warmth was because she'd told him she had to be back at O'Mara's for two o'clock as she had a Canadian tour party arriving. She liked to be on hand to meet their guests arriving, priding herself on the personal touch when it came to her role managing the family's guesthouse. She also knew her fiancé well enough to know if she arranged to meet him inside his bistro, he'd find something last minute that he had to do, that couldn't possibly wait. For his part he knew his intended well enough not to argue, not when she seemed to be walking a tight rope of nervous energy as their wedding drew nearer.

He reached her and wrapped her in a hello hug followed by a kiss and Aisling inhaled the familiar scent of cooking that clung to him along with the aftershave she'd bought him for his birthday. It was a warm and spicy scent that did peculiar things to her, things that were not suitable to be thinking about when one had a threesome with the bank manager planned.

'All set?' Quinn asked, releasing her and offering her his arm.

'All set,' she said, linking her arm through his and putting her best foot forward.

THE QUEUE, GIVEN PEOPLE were on their lunch breaks, was to the door and Aisling was glad they had an appointment. She hated queuing; it seemed like such a complete waste of time, especially with her impending nuptials which meant she had one hundred and one other things she could be doing at any given time along with all her ordinary day to day tasks. They were led through to a tiny waiting room and told by a bored looking woman that Mr Cleary shouldn't be long.'

No tea or coffee was on offer then, Aisling thought, glancing around before sitting down.

Quinn perched next to her muttering, 'It's a power play thing. 'He's letting us know his time's more precious than ours.' He was working his hands, and Aisling realised he was anxious. She took hold of them and gave them a reassuring squeeze before looking about for a magazine to flick through. You never knew your luck, there might be a Bridal Today lurking or the like. There were none, only a rack of pamphlets pertaining to banking with smiley, happy people who were all saving hard on the glossy covers.

A lonely water cooler gurgled away like a hungry tummy in the corner of the closet-like space. They were a tight old lot these bankers, she thought, trying to picture Mr Cleary. 'I bet yer man in there,' she said, pointing to the closed door with its gold nameplate, 'is small and yappy like a Jack Russell.'

Her comment made Quinn smile. It was then she remembered the brochure she'd tucked in her bag. Now was as good a time to mention what she had a feeling was going to be a hard sell. It was time to talk honeymoon and given she'd worked in resort management for years, she had her heart set on something completely out of the box to the sunshine playgrounds she'd spent so much time in. She retrieved the brochure and passed it over to him asking, 'What do you think of this then?'

Quinn stared at it, frowning, before stating the obvious. 'It's a hotel made of ice.'

'I know that,' Aisling laughed. 'It's the Ice Hotel, you eejit. You know the one that's carved every year from blocks of the stuff up the top of Sweden. It's been on the tele.'

'Why?'

'Why what?'

'Why do they do it?'

'Because it's beautiful and it's unique, that's why. Every single thing right down to the glasses used in the hotel bar is carved from ice. Imagine it, Quinn.' Her smile was dreamy as she pictured the winter wonderland of Narnia. She'd lost herself in there many times as a child when she'd hidden away at the back of her wardrobe trying to find a secret doorway.

'Okay, it's erm, very creative but why are you showing me this?' Quinn had a feeling he knew where this conversation was headed.

'I think we should have our honeymoon there. That's why.'

He'd guessed right and shivered at the very thought of it. 'Won't it be a tad chilly though?'

'Well, you don't get around in your swimming trunks. You have to have the proper winter gear but sure, look,' she took the brochure from him and flicked through to a picture of a couple looking deliriously happy as they snuggled together under reindeer skins despite lying on a bed carved of ice.

'They've got hats on.' Quinn pointed out. 'And I bet they've got socks on too. I didn't picture myself wearing a hat and socks to bed on my honeymoon or freezing my arse off on a bed made of ice for that matter.'

'There's such a thing as body heat.' Aisling waggled her eyebrows at him.

'There is that.' He grinned.

Sensing weakness she warmed to her theme. 'And, it's not *just* a hotel.'

'I can see that. It's a fecking igloo too.'

She elbowed him. 'It's a living breathing ice art gallery.' She'd stolen that bit from the small print in the brochure. 'Imagine telling our children that's where we spent our honeymoon.'

'What children? My little swimmers will be frozen forever if you make me go there.'

'We could sip schnapps that would warm them back up and watch the Northern Lights.'

'Isn't it the Germans who drink schnapps?'

'The Swedes do too, I looked it up, but alright then, we'll have a hot toddy of Swedish glogg if it makes you happy.'

He looked at her blankly.

'It's like mulled wine.'

'Ah.' He liked the mulled wine and the body heat side of things but he was still having a hard time with the hats and socks.

'We could go for a sled ride through the pine forest too.'

'And will Rudolph be there, Aisling?'

'Ha ha, it's huskies that pull the sleds not reindeer.'

Quinn could see he was fighting a losing battle. It wasn't looking likely she'd agree to the B&B in Kerry he'd been going to suggest and he wanted to keep his bride happy. He played his last card even though he knew he'd lost. 'It looks expensive.'

Aisling laid down her hand and it was a blinder. 'It's not that bad when you think of what an experience it will be. What price do you put on a memory that will last us a lifetime, Quinn?'

'Feck it, Aisling, you'd better by me some thermal socks, then. And if they do a budget ice suite that's the one you're too book, alright?'

'Yay!' Aisling gave a little cheer before planting a sloppy kiss on his cheek. 'Don't you worry,' she said, giving his thigh a meaningful squeeze 'I'll make sure you have a good time, big boy. You won't feel the cold on my bedtime watch.'

Quinn coughed, 'Er, Ash.'

She looked over to see Mr Cleary, not quite a snappy Jack Russell more of a droopy eyed bloodhound, standing in the doorway of his office.

'If you'd like to come in, when you're ready,' he said, giving a little cough.

Chapter 2

Two days had passed since Quinn and Aisling's successful visit to the bank. Despite the less than auspicious start, Mr Cleary, who had insisted they call him Michael, had been quite accommodating in the end and they'd left with the promise of sizable loan when the time came and a brand spanking new account in both their names. Now though, the good mood Aisling had been floating about in at the thought of stargazing near the North Pole was dissipating. To be blunt, Aisling O'Mara was in foul humour. She could hear Mammy's voice in her head telling her, 'You always are a moody madam when you're hungry.' And, Aisling was hungry.

She eyed Bronagh's drawer, the guesthouse's receptionist had nipped to the loo and the custard creams she knew Bronagh had tucked away in there called to her. *Eat me, eat me, eat me, Aisling,* they whispered. It was like a scene from the *Little Shop of Horrors*, so it was. She glanced toward the bathroom and saw the door still closed. Her hand reached forward and grasped the knob of the drawer but the sudden glint of blue light saw her snatch it back as though burned.

A diamond solitaire engagement ring, oval cut set in white gold no less, was better than any Weight Watchers meeting or Slimmer's Club get together. The most beautiful thing she'd ever been given in her life was right there on her ring finger reminding her that in a few weeks, she, Aisling Elizabeth O'Mara would become Mrs Aisling O'Mara-Moran. *How many times had she practiced introducing herself like that these last few weeks? Yes, hello there I'm Mrs O'Mara-Moran. Mrs O'Mara-Moran is the name. Aisling, Aisling O'Mara-Moran pleased to make your acquaintance.* For some reason when she said it in her head, she sounded posh, plummy like Joanna Lumley. She thought it might be because she was going to be the proud owner of a double-barrelled surname.

Mammy had been perturbed when Aisling had said she wanted to keep the O'Mara. 'Aisling that's the sort of modern thing Moira would do to be different,' she'd said and Aisling had replied. 'It's for Daddy, Mammy. I want to carry on our sur-name for him.' She didn't add that her brother, Patrick was over in America so he was hardly doing his bit for carrying on the O'Mara name in Ireland. Mammy had cried hearing this and said Aisling was a wonderful daughter. Five minutes later she'd accused her of eating the last Snowball she'd been saving and had planned on savouring as she watched Ballykissangel later that evening. Aisling had said she wouldn't and hadn't but the coconut flakes on her sweater had given her away.

'What are you doing?' Bronagh's waspish voice made her jump.

'Nothing. I was about to go through the diary to see what guests we've got arriving today, that's all.'

The receptionist's dark eyes narrowed. 'I know what was on your mind. I can read you like a book so I can, and you'll not find any biscuits in there. I've hidden them. I'll not have it on my head when the zip gets stuck halfway up your back on your big day. Nobody will be able to say Bronagh Hanrahan had her own best interests at heart. Or accuse me of sabotaging your chance to lose weight for my own financial gain.'

Aisling tried to look innocent, hoping the rapid blinking and widening of her eyes would convince Bronagh she'd not been planning a custard cream biscuit heist. 'I've lost three pounds. I'm on track, thank you very much and have no interest in sweets of any sort.' The Pope himself would be proud of how pious she sounded.

Bronagh patted her middle; the fabric of her skirt was shiny and stretched tight. 'I've lost three and a half pounds myself and I have to say I'm feeling marvellous for it. And, remember I've the menopause to do battle with too.'

Bronagh must be going through the longest running menopause on record, Aisling thought and her skirt didn't look any looser than it had done last week. She reckoned it was a tactic and Bronagh was trying to psych her out. They eyed one another. She was very competitive was Bronagh, Aisling thought. This silly competition was all down to her too because as soon as Aisling announced she wanted to lose half a stone for her wedding, Bronagh had been all for putting money on who'd reach their target weight first. She said it would keep them motivated if they were dieting for high stakes. Aisling would have been content with sticking a photo of Cindy Crawford in her swimsuit on the fridge but Moira had been lurking in the background and it was her that had egged them both on. Sure, it had been like a scene from a women's prison with her little sister's carry-on. She might as well have been yelling, 'Fight, fight, fight!'

Aisling was not one to back down from a challenge and in the end, she'd wagered a tenner that it would be her that lost her poundage first. After all, the odds were in her favour given it was her wedding she wanted to be in fine fettle for. Moira having already cleared it with Aisling that she would not be paying for her bridesmaid dress – given she was a poor student, but that in no way meant she'd wear some frothy pink ensemble and look like an eejit either – had seen a way to supplement her income instantly. She was running a book on the great weight loss race. So far, Aisling was the favourite but, Moira had stated over her toast that morning watching as Aisling lovingly ca-ressed the honey jar, it could change, just like that. She'd clicked her fingers for effect and Aisling had shoved the pot back in the cupboard and retrieved the Marmite instead.

'Have you done the stairs this morning?' Aisling asked Bronagh.

Moira had also taken it upon herself to be both women's personal trainer. Neither had asked her to do this and as such when she'd asked for payment for services rendered, they'd both told her to feck off. She'd not given up though and had said she'd do it out of the goodness of her heart. When she'd appeared in reception in joggers with a whistle around her neck both women had told her to feck off once more, but to no avail. In the end, Bronagh had climbed the stairs on the condition Moira hand over the whistle. She'd hidden it like she had the custard creams.

'I have. Moira made me do it before she left for college. It wasn't easy in this skirt I can tell you but I made it to the top floor with no rests, that's a first for me. What about yourself?'

'She's got me booked for a session after dinner.' Aisling frowned. To avoid temptation at Quinn's she'd been eating her meals here at O'Mara's under the watchful eye of Moira. She was fed up to the back teeth with salad and lean meat or vegetables and lean meat. She wanted a great big burger with fries, lots of skinny fries. *Stop it, Aisling.*

The door to the guesthouse opened and it was a welcome distraction to watch a giant bouquet of flowers with legs walk toward them. It was their fortnightly arrangement of blooms for the reception desk from Fi's Florists and Aisling recognised young Caitlin, Fi's new apprentice's voice as she said good morning to them both.

'Here I'll take those, Caitlin, they're gorgeous. Did you arrange them?' Aisling took the flowers and inhaled the sweet aroma from the gardenias. Were they edible, she wondered, and would she have gardenias in her bridal bouquet? She filed the latter question away to bring up with Leila when they met for lunch or in her case lettuce leaves.

'I did, thanks. How're the wedding plans coming along, Aisling? It's not long to go now.' The young girl's cheeks were flushed from the cold outside and the tip of her nose bright red; she sneezed.

'Bless you.' Bronagh immediately said.

'Sorry, I've a bit of a sniffle.'

Aisling took a step back, she could not afford to get sick, not now when she had so much on her plate (a bad choice of metaphor), she decided. 'Grand, thanks, Caitlin. Everything's coming along nicely.' She liked to think the more she said this the more she'd believe it. The power of positive thinking and all that.

Bronagh put her hand up to her mouth and mouthed, 'She's a complete nightmare.' to Caitlin who grinned.

'Well I'd best be off and carry on with my rounds.'

'Thanks very much,' Aisling called over her shoulder, carrying the flowers through to the kitchen. The guest's lounge room was empty and she made a note to self to replenish the tea and coffee sachets once she'd sorted the bouquet. She always found the act of placing the fresh flowers in the vase therapeutic and hopefully it would improve her mood. She didn't like being snappy and edgy; it wasn't like her and it wasn't all down to the fact she was about to start gnawing on her arm if she didn't get some sustenance in her shortly. It was her own fault. She'd set a ridiculously tight timeframe in which to organise her wedding. Everybody thought she was mad. Quinn included. They'd gotten engaged on Christmas Day and now here she was expecting to have a big, white wedding with all the trimmings on the fourteenth of February, Valentine's Day, no less.

It had given her shy of eight weeks in which to organise everything. Thank the Lord for Leila. The gods had smiled down on her the day her best friend had decided to launch her own wedding planner business. This wedding would be a rip-roaring success because Love Leila Bridal Planning services was backing her all the way. Sure, if it weren't for Leila, she'd be headed straight for the registry office dragging Quinn along behind her. Leila had the power to get them in with places that otherwise would have told them to come back in a year when they had space free in the diary. Of course, it wasn't the first time Leila had planned a wedding for her which was why Aisling had no intention of dilly-dallying for a year while all the arrangements were made. Sure, anything could happen like it had once before. She'd been let down weeks out from her wedding, which obviously was a blessing as, with the benefit of hindsight, her ex-fiancé was an eejit of the highest order. It hadn't felt like a blessing at the time though. It had been the most humiliating experience of her life.

Oh, she knew right enough Quinn wouldn't let her down but there was still the fear. The omnipresent fear she couldn't shake that unless she expedited matters something would go wrong. She sighed, and filled the vase. She should be feeling excited and full of the joys of being a bride-to-be. Instead she was an anxious, hungry wreck. She began to pen one of her imaginary letters, something she hadn't done in a long time.

Dear Aisling,

I'm getting married soon and I want to know how I can make this gnawing feeling in the pit of my stomach go away, and please don't tell me to eat a lovely, great big slice of chocolate cake with fresh cream filling and a ganache icing because that won't help.

Yours faithfully,

Me

Chapter 3

'Aisling have you had any further thoughts on the reception's seating arrangements?' Maureen O'Mara asked her daughter.

'Leila and I were going to go over those again at lunchtime, why?' Aisling knew she was going to regret asking like she was already regretting having answered the phone. Mammy was driving her round the bend with her daily guestlist updates. She'd only nipped upstairs for a quick sandwich before she headed out to meet Leila. It was not on her to-do list to sit and listen to Mammy gabble on about who wouldn't be seated next to whom and who was allergic to what. She'd already been delayed by having to sort Ita out on her way upstairs.

She'd spotted their self-titled Director of Housekeeping on the first-floor landing. She'd been pretending to look for supplies in the cupboard at the end of the hall where all the cleaning products were kept. Aisling had tiptoed toward her, guessing she was engrossed in a game on her phone. 'Ita, could you make up room six please. The Fenchurch family are arriving within the hour and they need the cot as well,' she'd said, in a voice designed to let her know she knew exactly what she'd been up to.

Ita had banged her head on the shelf above her and hastily shoved her phone back in the pocket of her smock. She'd picked up a bottle of detergent before scurrying off with a wounded look on her face. It had annoyed Aisling that she should be made to feel guilty over the way she'd spoken to her and she'd stomped up the rest of the stairs to the family's apartment on the top floor wishing she could be made of sterner stuff, like Moira.

If it had been the youngest O'Mara, she'd have told Ita to get off her idle arse and get on with the job she was being paid to do without so much as a second thought. Aisling had set about slapping two pieces of soft, white bread together, sandwiching the thick spread of honey between them as the telephone had begun to shrill. She knew who it would be before she picked up but she also knew from experience that it did no good ignoring Mammy, she'd track you down eventually.

Now, she flopped down on the armchair by the window and took a deep breath. The light doing its best to shine in through the windows was weak and wintery but at least it wasn't raining. She sniffed; it smelt a bit doggy in here. That was down to Pooh. She'd have to spray the air freshener about the place. Mammy was after buying her a can in order to stop her complaining about her bringing the poodle to visit. The downside of this was she'd bought the one that smelled like her favourite perfume, Arpège, so now the apartment either smelled of poodle or Mammy. She kept looking over her shoulder expecting to see one or both of them lurking in the shadows.

She took a bite of her honey sandwich and the sweet burst on her tongue was comforting. She chewed as Mammy informed her, 'I'm after hearing from your great aunt Noreen down in that godforsaken place she lives in again. I think they only got the electricity last year. In a right state she was. She says she won't enjoy her meal if she's put at the same table as your aunt Emer. There's bad blood between those two, not that anybody knows why. Although I'm sure Emer's mammy, Rosamunde, knows what's gone on but she's not saying. Anyway, Noreen says she'll not be held responsible for her actions if Emer winds up next to her. Your father's side of the family always were a pain in the arse except for his mammy and da, God rest their souls.' she sniffed.

Noreen wasn't technically Aisling's great aunt at all. It was all very complicated but from memory she was her dad's cousin the correct title as to what that made her to Aisling a mystery so great aunt it was. She rolled her eyes at the thought of the old biddy laying down the law to Mammy. 'The only reason your side wasn't a pain in the arse too was because you'd fallen out with them, Mammy and we never saw them.' Aisling sighed because unfortunately her mammy's brothers were making up for lost time now and had all informed their sister they were waiting for their invitations to their favourite niece's wedding. Sure, she'd only met them a handful of times. The politics of planning a wedding were all very frustrating.

'I am not a one-woman United Nations you know,' Aisling said, thinking about how Uncle Brendan had threatened to clock Uncle Frankie if he mouthed off at the reception. It was a likely scenario given Frankie's love of a drop. 'To be honest, I don't know why your brothers have to come at all, Mammy. Tom will sit there picking his nose all through the speeches like he did at Rosi's wedding and Colm couldn't keep his hands to himself with any of her friends. Disgusting he was, following the girls half his age around saying, 'Now then, how's about a kiss for the bride's uncle? As for Brendan and Frankie it will be fisticuffs at dawn mark my words.' Aisling put her hand on her chest; she could feel her heart beginning to pump a little faster at the stress of it all. 'It's not as if we ever see any of them either. And what about Cousin Jackie and her shellfish allergy, not to mention Aunt Ina who doesn't want to be seated near the band because she won't be able to hear herself think. I'm pulling my hair out here.'

'Ah now, Aisling, calm down. My brothers are heathens I'll grant you but I've no parents left in this world and family is family. Your day will be grand so it will and all this will be a storm in a teacup like the KY2 business at New Year.'

Aisling frowned, surely Mammy wasn't on about a new version of an old favourite that a girl's mammy should know nothing about in the first place – and then the penny dropped. 'Oh, you mean the Y2K bug.'

'Yes, that. Why, what did you think I meant?'

'Erm never mind.'

'Well you get my point, Aisling. We saw the millennium in with fireworks galore but despite all the merchants of doom predicting the world as we knew it was going to crash down around us, it didn't. Sure, it'll be the same with your wedding. There'll be a few crackers going off but no major catastrophes. Mark my words.'

Aisling wasn't sure she liked her impending nuptials being compared to the Millennium bug and she'd prefer it if no crackers went off thanks very much but Mammy had only paused to draw breath so she didn't get a chance to protest. 'Have you heard back from Cormac as to whether he's coming over from America to walk you down the aisle.'

Cormac was her dad's older brother. Aisling had gotten to know him when she'd visited LA on stopovers to her various resort postings. Her dad had never spoken about him much when they were growing up. There were nearly ten years between them and Cormac had left home and sailed to America in search of adventure and to make his fortune, or so Daddy had always said, when he was still a young lad. He'd done well for himself, becoming a mover and shaker in the LA fashion scene where he'd wound up making his home. From a grown-up perspective, Aisling had concluded that what had driven Uncle Cormac to America all those years ago was not the need for adventure but a need for acceptance, something his effeminate ways would have struggled to find in Ireland when he was a younger man

When the time had come, he'd had no interest in taking over the running of the family's guesthouse. So, it had fallen to his younger brother, Aisling's daddy, Brian. Her brother Patrick caught up with Cormac from time to time over there in the city of angels but apart from funerals, and weddings the rest of the family hardly saw him. It had been Mammy's bright idea to have Cormac give her away when she was supposed to walk down the aisle the first time around. A stand in for Daddy. Tears prickled and she blinked them away because more than anything she wished her dad could be the one whose arm she linked hers through as he led her down the aisle to meet Quinn. She liked to think he'd be there in spirit. Cormac was no Daddy but she was very fond of him. He was their closest male blood relative excluding her mammy's brothers and Patrick and the thought of any of them marching her up the aisle was enough to bring her out in a rash.

She'd felt sheepish when she'd telephoned Cormac a second time to ask if he would do her this favour. His relaxed drawl made her think of blond shaggy-haired surfer dudes and hum Beach Boy tunes whereas in reality Uncle Cormac was a short man whose fondness for the finer things in life saw his belly rest comfortably over the top of the flowing, loose fitting linen pants he favoured. She also suspected he wore a toupee. A very good one, granted. They made good ones in LA. Uncle Cormac, with his tendency to talk with those beringed hands of his was one of life's characters, Aisling had decided long ago and without him the world would be a little duller.

He hadn't beaten around the bush, telling her he wanted to check out travel insurance policies for their cancellation clauses this time around before saying yes, given he'd not been able to get a refund on his flights the last time she'd been going to get married.

He'd telephoned her the other day and she'd thought she'd passed the news on to Mammy that yes, he would be there and to make a room up for him at the guesthouse. It must have slipped her mind. She informed Mammy of his call.

'The reason you're forgetting things, Aisling, is because you've too much on your plate.'

Aisling thought that was an ironic thing to say, given there'd been feck all on her plate since she'd started her weight-loss journey, or nightmare, whichever way you wanted to look at it.

'And,' Maureen said, failing to see any irony in her words whatsoever. 'I understand the planning of your big day is a stressful thing but that's what the mother of the bride is for. It is my job to be a good listener, constant giver of compliments, cheerleader, and source of support to you.'

'Mammy, are you reading that out?'

'No, I am not.'

'You are too.'

'Well, according to Bridal Life magazine that's my role and as such I want you to know you can relax because I've had a grand idea. Why don't I come along for the luncheon with you and Leila? I don't mind cancelling my watercolour workshop this afternoon. I'm annoyed with Rosemary Farrell anyway and could happily give it a miss. She's after copying my idea of doing a self-portrait. You want to see hers, Aisling, she looks like yer wan with her gob wide open in that painting Moira was after putting on her wall as a teenager. Jaysus it gave us all nightmares so it did.'

Aisling knew the painting Mammy was talking about. 'Edvard Munch's, *The Scream*. He was a Norwegian expressionist.' She spieled off the explanation Moira had given them all for the disturbing print she'd hung in pride of place on her bedroom wall. It had frightened Aisling almost as much as the Bono poster her little sister used to stick to her bedroom door as payback for something or other. 'She told us we were all heathens who wouldn't know great art if it smacked us in the head.'

'So, she did. Uppity wee madam she was in her teens. Terrible phase. Anyway, what I was saying is that I could fill Leila in on all the family and who's to go where. Take a load off of it all for you.'

'No, thank you, Mammy. We'll manage.' Aisling knew her mammy was itching to take over from Leila; she'd done exactly that with Roisin's wedding and if she were to give her an inch, she'd take a mile. 'You're in charge of the RSVPs sure, and you and Bronagh are having to sort out who's staying in what room.' No guest bookings were to be taken two days prior or after the wedding. 'That's a big enough responsibility.' She'd given Mammy the task of tallying up who was coming and sorting out accommodations because she wanted her to feel part of it all, but that was a big enough part, thank you very much.

'Well it is when you only give people a few weeks' notice, Aisling.'

'Mammy, we've been through all of this. I don't see the point in dragging things out.'

'There's dragging things out and then there's your Shogun wedding. People will talk.'

'Shotgun wedding, Mammy. People don't have to get married anymore because they've a baby on the way but for the record, I'm not in the family way thanks very much. So, people can talk all they like.'

'Aisling, have you something in your mouth?'

'No, of course not.' She swallowed the bite of her sandwich.

'Aisling O'Mara, your nose grew then so it did. And don't you come crying to me when you're a tenner short and your dress won't fit.'

Aisling scowled and dropped what was left of the sandwich back on the plate. 'Look, Mammy, I've got to go.'

'Well, don't let me hold you up. I'm only your mammy after all.'

Aisling rolled her eyes; spare her the poor, hard done by Mammy act. 'Bye-bye, enjoy your watercolour painting class.' As Aisling hung up, a thought popped into her head. She hoped Mammy wasn't after doing a self-portrait as a wedding present for her and Quinn. Jaysus! Her grinning down at them as they lay in their marital bed would give her nightmares and be the end of any riding. She wrapped herself inside her coat and picked up her bag, her eyes alighting on her book, open to where she'd left it on the coffee table the night before. Roisin had given her it for Christmas and she'd managed to read two more chapters before her eyes had grown heavy. The next thing she'd known, Moira was nudging her telling her to feck off to bed because she couldn't hear the tele over her snoring. What she wouldn't give to clamber back into bed now with a nice cup of tea and a plate of hot buttered toast. Oh, to while away the afternoon with her book. Her idea of bliss. Give her that any day over an upmarket spa, she thought as she headed out the door making a mental note to self to get Moira to start giving her weekly facials and to be sure to double check her manicurist appointment and, somewhere in between her list of one hundred and one things to do, she'd have to find time to see her fiancé.

Chapter 4

Noreen

Noreen Grady's knitting needles clicked and clacked to a rhythm of their own. She was knitting a jersey for the sick babies in Africa. It was a vibrant affair of yellow and orange because she thought the little baby who wore it would like the bright, cheery colour. Another twenty minutes and she'd have it done. Then she could put it in Kathleen's box along with the others waiting to be shipped off to the hospital in South Africa. Agnes, Margaret and Kathleen, with whom she met each Friday here at Alma's Tea Shop to catch up on all the week's news while they all did their bit for those less fortunate than themselves, were also clacking away. Once the jerseys were finished, they were going to start on hats for the little prem babies at the hospital in Cork.

Her three friends were in the midst of a whispered discussion over whether Alma's currant buns had been on the dry side and was she after putting yesterday's buns back in the cabinet? Noreen thought it quite likely. She was a business woman herself and Alma was as hard-nosed and sharp as they came, didn't miss a trick.

The jangle of the door opening brought in a whiff of cigarette smoke from a smouldering fag end on the pavement outside. The jangling was a sound that always took her back to her own days behind the counter. It was a familiar tinkle, signalling someone was in need of something, and had always seen her put down the tins she was restocking the shelves with or whatever she'd been busy doing to look up and say a cheery hello. Alma could do with injecting a little more of the cheer into her greeting, she thought looking at the po-faced woman as she wiped out her cabinets. Noreen missed running her little corner shop. It hadn't just been a place to get your essentials it had been a hub for hearing all about what was happening in the village of Claredoncally where she'd lived for all of her married life.

Things were changing here though, she thought, as a truck rumbled through the narrow street outside. The windows rattled and her seat juddered. Oh, they were changing alright and not for the better in her opinion. Her shop was a Spar now. A Spar! Who'd have thought. All the personality and personal service she and her late husband, Malachy, God rest his poor departed soul, prided themselves on, leached from it by a generic chain store. It had been their child that shop. They'd poured the love and energy left over from not being able to have a baby of their own into it. And it had been enough too, almost. The hole still left by the absence of children's laughter had been filled by Emer. It had broken her heart to take down the sign they'd hung over the door some fifty years earlier almost as much as it had broken her heart when Malachy passed. But passed he had and practical she had to be. She was no longer able to manage the stairs to the cosy home they'd made above the shop. The time had come to put her feet up.

The price for the premises dangled under her nose by the conglomerate was the sort that didn't come along twice and so, despite her misgivings at accepting, common sense had been the order of the day. She liked to think Malachy would have approved, or at least understood. The business and home didn't fit anymore with him gone. It had become too much to manage for a widow woman on her own.

It had been an adjustment to move into the brand new, little house she'd had built on an empty square parcel of land three streets down from the main road of Claredoncally. It was quieter for one thing, especially with the double glazing on the windows. There was something to be said for a few mod cons and creature comforts in one's old age though, and her chest at least hadn't missed the damp beginning to seep through the walls of the bathroom in the rooms above the shop.

She hoped Malachy was having a good long rest up there with the angels. He deserved it, he'd worked hard all his life. Never harder than when they were young. Fresh out of the high school they'd both gone off to earn their keep at the local fish factory, saving what pennies were left from their board to go toward their wedding and their dream of buying Mr Brosnan's corner shop when the time came. Sure, everybody had known the old man was going doolally from the way he kept handing out too much or too little change and talking about the oddest of things, yes it had been high time he sold up. And, when he did, they'd been ready and so the little corner shop in charge of servicing the village of Claredoncally had become Grady's Convenience Store.

She'd felt such pride in the place and had never tired of turning the sign hanging in the window from closed to open. There was no greater satisfaction than being one's own boss in life. She smiled to herself, recalling how she and Malachy used to laugh about how nice it was to finish their days work with him not smelling like a mackerel, her a herring. And, they never ate fish ever again except when they had to, as good Catholics, on a Friday.

'*Noreen*,' there was irritation in Kathleen's voice and Noreen looked at her blankly, coming back from her reminiscing to ask her old friend to repeat what she'd said.

'Sure, you were away with the fairies. I asked you about this big do in Dublin, Aggie's after telling me you're off to.'

'Oh yes, the wedding.' Noreen put her knitting down; she'd been trying not to think about it. She looked at the teapot on the table. Another strong cup of tea was in order if she were to relay this tale. 'Any chance of more hot water, Alma,' she called. Alma nodded, muttering something under her breath as she put her cloth down and set about filling the kettle.

'Can I interest you in another currant bun each? They'd go down a treat with your tea,' she asked, waddling over and setting the water down.

'Sure, you'd need something to wash them down. Stick in your gullet those would,' Agnes muttered.

'What did you say, Aggie?' Alma said, wincing. 'My knees aren't half giving me bother today.' Her expression was a grimace as Agnes shook her head but didn't bother to repeat her sentiment. 'It's no good for my arthritis all this standing about. I'm too old for this lark.'

'Giving the buns, away are you?' Margaret ignored her moans and groans never pausing in her purl stitch.

'You want to take a leaf out of my book, Alma, and retire,' Noreen offered up.

'Sure, and how am I supposed to afford the likes of putting my feet up when Margaret here would have me giving away my earnings. She'd have me in the poor house.'

'Ah, get away with you. I'll have a bun but heat it up would you and for the love of God put some butter on it,' Agnes said, and Alma scuttled off before she could change her mind. Noreen topped up the pot and while she waited for the tea to steep, she filled her three friends in on the invitation she'd received a few days ago.

'So, the wedding is at the family's church there in Dublin and the reception is to be held at the restaurant her fiancé owns. And you'll be accommodated at the guesthouse your grand-niece or whatever she is runs,' Kathleen clarified. None of the women had been able to come up with an appropriate title for the daughter of a cousin either so grand-niece it was.

Noreen nodded.

'Well for someone who won't have to lift a finger for a few days you don't look very happy about it all,' Agnes pointed out.

'Is it Emer?' Kathleen asked, studying Noreen's face, knowing the family history. 'Will she be there?'

Noreen's lips tightened at the mention of her sister's child, Emer, who she'd taken under her wing. Emer, who she'd treated like a daughter. Emer, who'd betrayed her.

'Yes,' she nodded. 'She will.'

Chapter 5

'Aisling, eat something would you,' Leila said, watching her friend play with her food across the table. She'd have preferred to go to Quinn's for lunch but Aisling had suggested they come here to Holy Moly the self-proclaimed salad gurus of Dublin instead. The only reason Aisling wanted to steer clear of her fiancé's bistro was because she knew he'd ignore her dietary requirements and present her with a plate heaped full of her favourite, bangers 'n' mash. Quinn, Aisling had confided in Leila, did not make her efforts to lose weight before the wedding easy. Aisling, Quinn had confided in Leila, was a nightmare when she was hungry and he wished she'd buy a dress in the next size up and be done with it.

'I don't like chickpeas.' Aisling speared one viciously with her fork before eying it as though it were a cyanide pill.

'Then why did you order a Moroccan salad?'

'Because it sounded exotic but healthy. I'd have rather have had what you're having but I didn't want all the garlicy, mayonnaise stuff. Perhaps I should have asked for it without the dressing.'

Leila had chosen the chicken Caesar salad and was thoroughly enjoying it. 'Yes, but if you don't have the dressing, it doesn't *taste* like a Caesar salad which defeats the purpose. Here have some croutons.' She flicked a couple over onto Aisling's plate.

Aisling crunched on them and then helped herself to a few more until Leila thwacked her with her fork. 'Leave some for me.'

'Sorry.' It wasn't fair Aisling lamented. Leila was a petite blue-eyed blonde who could stuff as many croutons and the like down her as she wanted and never gain a pound. Sure, all *she* had to do was sniff anything remotely tasty and it took up residence on her hips. She debated briefly as to whether she should risk one more, crispy piece of the dried bread but then decided no, she'd crack on with what they'd come here to talk about. It would take her mind off eating, for the interim at any rate. 'I don't want anything to be the same, Leila. Not one single thing. You know that don't you?'

'As when you were planning to marry Marcus the Fecker McDonagh? Yes, Aisling, you've mentioned it more than once.'

'Exactly.' She waved her fork at her friend and the chickpea fell back into the bowl. 'I'm not shopping at Ivory Bridal Couture this time around either because I think it jinxed me the last time.'

'The only thing jinxing you was that ex-fecker of a fiancé of yours and good riddance to him.'

Aisling agreed with the latter sentiment. 'I know, if Marcus hadn't jilted me then I wouldn't have gotten together with Quinn but I'm not taking any chances, Leila. I've booked us an appointment at Bridal Emporium on Friday afternoon, which, as you know is a one-stop shop for the bride, the bridesmaid, and the mother of the bride, then on the Saturday we've an appointment at Hair She Goes to figure out how we're all going to be wearing our hair. I texted you the times, did you get it? It's going to be a busy weekend.'

Leila held a hand up. 'You're speaking way too fast, Aisling. Slow down and take a deep breath.'

Aisling knew she was beginning to sound like one of the Chipmunks whenever she talked about her wedding but she couldn't help it. She inhaled slowly through her nose and out through her mouth like Roisin had showed her. It helped a little.

Leila carried on. 'It is going to be busy, but sure, it's great Rosi's coming over to be part of it all.'

'Yes, she can help me keep Mammy in line. I think Mammy's feeling a little left out of things but one of the reasons I chose Bridal Emporium was so she'll be occupied choosing her mammy of the bride outfit instead of focussing on my dress. Do you remember, Roisin's?'

'I do.' Leila said sobering at the memory of the white crochet toilet dolly dress, Roisin had been lumbered with in order to keep her mammy happy. Then, thinking of Maureen O'Mara sitting all alone in her apartment in Howth when she could be joining them for lunch added, 'Poor Maureen. You should have brought her along with you today, Aisling. She could have been brought up to speed with all the plans.'

'There's not shutting her out and being a complete roll-over, Leila.'

'True.'

They giggled. 'Anyway, enough about Mammy. I want a completely different style of dress this time and need you there to be honest with me but in a nice way, okay?' She pinned her gaze on her friend, already hearing Moira in her head, '*It makes you look like a milk bottle with a red top and freckles, Ash, get it off.*'

Leila raised two fingers to her temple, 'I promise to do my best, Brownie's honour.' Her smile however drooped at the re-alisation Aisling's insistence everything be different this time around meant she could say goodbye to the beautiful brides-maids' dresses previously picked out.

Aisling registered the disappointed look on her friend's face. 'I'm sorry, Leila, I know you look gorgeous in soft blue but we're going for a whole new look for all of us. I don't want any reminders, okay?'

'Fair play to you, although they were divine. You don't have to pay for mine either. You're spending enough as it is and, speaking of money...'

Were they? Aisling thought finding the topic distasteful.

'I am keeping a running total of your expenditure, here.' Leila produced a notebook in which was a handwritten tally of columns with deposits put down and a note as to the balance and when it was due. She pushed it toward Aisling who gazed at it blankly before sliding it back to Leila.

'It's a good idea to check-in with this regularly, Ash. So you don't get any nasty surprises.' She snapped the book shut. 'It's amazing how costs for a wedding can escalate and these days bridesmaids don't expect the bride to cover their dresses.'

Aisling had no choice but to spring for Moira's dress and as such it was only fair she did the same for Roisin, who wasn't cashed up either. As for Leila, she was grateful to her for com-ing to the rescue with the organising of her day on such short notice. The dress was her way of saying thank you to her friend. 'I want to.'

'Well, I appreciate it, Ash, but promise me you won't go overboard alright? You're the star of the show. And we don't want anything short either, alright? Or, we'll all have fecking goosebumps in the photographs, and can we have a cape or jacket of some description so we don't freeze our arses off? I saw some horrendous photos of a winter wedding the other day where the bridal party was all lined up with the bridesmaids' headlights on full beam. Imagine passing it around the family?' She shuddered.

Aisling grimaced. 'Uncle Colm would love it! He'd probably ask if he could have the negatives.'

Leila laughed. She'd been targeted for a kiss from Uncle Colm on the dance floor at Roisin's wedding reception. 'And, are we still on for next Saturday night, too?'

Aisling nodded although she could do without it, to be honest. A hen night was at the bottom of her list of priorities but Moira had insisted on organising it and with Roisin coming to stay for the weekend, there was no getting out of it. 'Yes, and I've told Moira I will not be wearing an Alice band with glittery purple willies bobbing about on it, or carrying a blow-up doll called Seamus around town like she was planning last time around. I said we're all older, and wiser and I'd wear a veil at a push.'

'I don't blame you.' Leila smiled, knowing Aisling could say what she liked to Moira. It would make no difference and she'd organise exactly what she wanted regardless of her sister's wishes. She was glad because to be frank, Aisling was so tightly wound she could do with letting her hair down and having a little fun.

'How's Bazzer? He's definitely on board to do the photographs isn't he?' Aisling grinned across the table. He was in demand for his photography skills but thanks to Leila he'd fitted their date in and offered a discount. Leila had told her Bearach didn't come cheap, even with the discount, and she shouldn't feel obligated to use him because she was dating him. He didn't expect them to. Aisling had barely listened to her. She was focussed only on the fact he was one of the best in the city. Her justification for using a top gun at his game was the discount he was going to give them.

Leila scowled at her. '*Bearach* thank you, is grand. And don't you dare call him Bazzer on the day or he'll take loads of unflattering pics and still charge an astronomical fee. Repeat after me Bearach.'

'Bearach.' She followed it up with a whispered, 'Bazzer.' And got a kick under the table.

'Sorry, I can't seem to help myself. I don't know why because he doesn't look like a Barry.'

'Because he's Bearach.'

'Yes, but he might as well be seeing as it means Barry.'

'What's wrong with Barry anyhow?' Leila frowned popping a piece of chicken in her mouth.

'Do you Leila take the Bazzer?'

Leila couldn't help herself, she laughed. 'Don't make me laugh when I'm eating. I could choke and, alright, I get your point but we're hardly about to march down the aisle. And he's grand, thank you. Although I did want to ask your advice about something.' She noticed Aisling's gaze was fixated on the remainder of her croutons once more and she quickly forked them up along with the rest of her salad.

Aisling waited patiently for her to swallow, lamenting the loss of the croutons as she watched Leila chew.

'Bearach's asked me to go down to Connemara to meet his parents and I don't think it's a good idea.'

'Why not? Connemara's one of my favourite places in Ireland. It's beautiful.'

'I know that but, Aisling,' Leila voice had the intonation of an exasperated parent trying to explain something to a small child. 'Meeting your boyfriend's parents is akin to announcing your serious about their son and I'm not sure I am.'

This was news to Aisling, but then she had been self-absorbed of late.

'But you said everything was grand.'

'No, I said *he's* grand.'

Aisling studied her friend. She knew the signs well. As soon as the fellow she was stepping out with began to make noises about moving things along in their relationship, Leila got cold feet. 'I think you should go.'

'You do?'

'Yes. You need to take his invitation at face value and not analyse it. What do I always say to you?'

'Analysis is paralysis.' Leila recited; a good student.

'Go and enjoy the opportunity to sample the delights of Connemara. Spend some time with his family who are probably very nice people keen to get know the woman who's been spending time with their son. The only person reading more into the invitation, is you.'

Leila smoothed the serviette she'd unwittingly been folding. 'You're right. Thanks, Ash. You know if you ever get tired of running O'Mara's you'd make a grand counsellor.'

Aisling smiled. She was good at helping other people see things clearly. Unfortunately, it was a life skill which didn't extend itself to her own life. She didn't dwell on this though as Leila retrieved the wedding file from her bag and, pushing her plate to one side put it on the table. She was all business now, flicking through the various pages of notes and pictures clipped inside until she came to what she was looking for.

'I wanted to know what you thought of these themes for the table settings.' Leila slid the folder toward her friend and Aisling began to flick through the various cuttings of different ideas filed and clipped inside it.

'They're all gorgeous. You know me so well,' she sighed, pausing over one particularly lovely idea with pinecones, lots of flickering tealight candles and white hydrangeas 'This one's lovely, simple but elegant. Perfect for a winter wedding. What do you think?' Her expression darkened, 'Do you think the hydrangeas would set Rosi's hay fever off? And what if one of Mammy's eejity brothers gets drunk and knocks the candles over?' She began to chew at her thumbnail as she was assailed with a high drama, action packed vision, whereby Roisin was bent double with the sneezes and her uncles were running about the place brandishing fire extinguishers like they were trained assassins. 'Do you think the candles might be a recipe for disaster?'

'Ash, calm down. Remember your mantra, breathe. It's your day and Quinn's. You should have exactly what you want and not be worrying about anyone else. Get your thumb out of your mouth, would you. If you start biting your nails now, you'll have to have falsies put on.'

Aisling dropped her hand. 'You're right.' She took a calming breath as instructed. 'It's my wedding and I can have what I want.'

'And Quinn's,' Leila corrected.

'Yes, yes, his too. Can I take this with me to show him?'

'Of course you can.'

Aisling unclipped the picture and folded it in half before sliding it into her bag. 'Where are you at with securing the carriage?' She wanted to sit inside a horse drawn carriage and wave to the commoners like the Princess Diana and even yer Fergie one had. She'd been practising her wave in the bathroom mirror.

'I'm in talks with Fergus Muldoon. I've put a lot of work his way in the past so he should come to the party despite the short notice and give us a good price.'

'Grand, thanks, Leila. Can you ask him to make sure the carriage looks as much like a pumpkin as possible? Oh, and I don't want any mangy horses off the estate either.'

'I will. Sure, you'll have a fine pumpkin carriage drawn by dancing white horses. You'll be Cinderella on the way to meet her prince.'

Aisling smiled liking the analogy. Quinn was her Prince Charming and she would live happily ever after – she'd make damned sure of it even if it was the death of her.

Chapter 6

'Aisling O'Mara, the woman who has not only broken my heart but shattered it into a million tiny pieces!' Alasdair flounced forth as Aisling burst in through the door of Quinn's eager to escape the cold.

It was no good her being cold when she was trying to lose weight because it made her want to stuff things down like stodgy, rib-sticking dinners followed by creamy rice pudding, with a dollop of Mrs Baicu's jam to sweeten it. Ah Jaysus, her mouth was already watering.

'The Cathy to my Heathcliff. Are we destined to always be kept apart?' Alasdair began to hum Kate Bush's *Wuthering Heights* his hands fluttering to his heart.

Aisling laughed as she unwound her scarf. 'Get away with you. It's freezing out.'

His voice returned to its normal cadence as he held his hand out, 'Here let me take your coat.'

She unbelted it and divested herself of it, passing the coat to him along with her scarf. He draped them over his arm. 'Thanks. The fire looks lovely.' Her expression was wistful as her eyes drifted across the restaurant to the fireplace aglow with dancing orange flames. Several patrons were basking in its warmth, enjoying the ambience it created as they savoured their desserts.

'Well, why don't you pull up a chair and put your feet up for a while, Aisling – I have no idea how your careen about town the way you do in those shoes.' He looked pointedly at her black Miu Miu's with their impossible high heels which meant she came up to Alasdair's chin. Without them she'd be navel gazing. 'Although, I have to say they are gorgeous.'

'Thank you, they are my favourites.' It was a half-truth. She loved all her designer shoes and had spent a small fortune collecting them over the years. They were all her favourites. 'And I'd love to curl up over there.'

'With a glass of vino,' Alasdair said enticingly. 'A cheeky little red perhaps?'

'Oh, you're tempting me.'

'That's the idea. You know you're my favourite redhead.'

'Ah now, there's a fib if ever I heard one. The fella you were seeing last month, what was his name?'

'Jamie.'

'Yes, Jamie. I heard you telling him he was your favourite redhead.'

'Ah but the fellas come and go, you, Aisling, my one true love, you are a constant.'

'Flatterer.' She grinned. 'And I can't sit and drink wine not when I've a wedding to be organising. Speaking of which, is he back from the suppliers?' She inclined her head toward the kitchen.

'He is, you'll find him out the back prepping for tonight's service.'

She smiled her thanks and passed through the restaurant saying hello to Paula whose ponytail was flicking about the place as she cleared tables. A smattering of diners were dotted about the space lingering over their lunches even though they probably should have been back at the office long since. Her stomach rumbled at the lingering hearty smells and spying a man tucking into a bowl of Irish stew she fought the good fight not to pick up a piece of the crusty bread on the plate next to it. Oh, how she'd love to dunk it into his stew! *Think of your dress, Aisling. No pain, no gain. Cindy Crawford, Cindy Crawford,* she added for good measure. She pushed through the doors into the kitchen and narrowly missed being hit by a flying piece of carrot. 'Hey, watch it!'

'Sorry, Aisling,' the sous-chef, Tony said. 'I was aiming for him.' He pointed to Quinn who was laughing.

'What are you to up to?' she asked taking in the scene.

Quinn put down the piece of potato he'd been about to fire and held his hands up. 'Truce?'

'Truce, so long as I don't have to sweep it up.' Tony pointed at the handful of chopped vegetables on the floor.

Aisling could see she wasn't going to get an answer, besides it was obvious the pair had been having some sort of food fight and irritation pricked at her. Here she was run off her feet organising their wedding and yet Quinn had time to arse about in the kitchen. 'You need a shave, Quinn Moran,' she said, a little snappier than she'd intended as she noticed his blond whiskers glinting in the light.

He didn't notice her pique and homed in for a kiss causing her to squeal.

'You're all prickly!'

Quinn grinned wolfishly before rubbing his chin on her cheek.

'Get off, you'll give me a rash,' she said, pushing him away.

He admitted defeat and headed to the sink to wash his hands. 'You're a hard woman so you are, Aisling O'Mara. Now

then, is this a social visit or an official wedding visit?' He didn't
know why he was asking given he knew the answer already. Aisling lived and breathed the wedding – it was all she'd talked
about since they'd gotten engaged on Christmas Day. Truth
be told she was driving him a little mad because you'd think
they were Posh and Becks the way she was carrying on. He un-
derstood her insecurity where the wedding was concerned although it rankled she couldn't shake the anxiety her eejit-ex
Marcus had left her with. She should be able to move past what
had happened because she knew he'd never do anything to let
her down. For whatever reason though, she couldn't and had
insisted on a ridiculously tight window of time in which to organise their day. It wouldn't have been so bad if she was happy
to have a low-key affair but she wasn't, she wanted the works.
He turned the tap off and picked up the towel, drying his hands
off as she answered.

'I'm here on official wedding business,' Aisling said, rum-
maging in her bag and pulling out a piece of paper. She didn't
ask whether he had time to take a look at the photograph because if he had time for horsing around with Tony, he had time
to help her make an important decision. 'Here, have a look at
this. I've come from lunch with Leila and she showed me some
fabulous ideas for table settings but this was the one I liked the
best. What do you think?'

She waited, eager for his response, while he looked at the
picture.

'A wise man agrees to everything,' Tony said going back to
dicing his carrots.

It was a sentiment Aisling had to agree with.

However, it would seem Quinn wasn't feeling wise because instead of the expected, 'It looks great, Ash, go for it,' she was waiting to hear he pulled a face and said, 'It's a bit, you know?'

'What?'

'I don't know,' he shrugged, already sensing this was not going to go down well, but it was too late now. 'A little over the top, I guess.'

Aisling snatched the paper back inspecting it. She couldn't see what was over the top about it. It was beautiful was what it was.

'Sorry, Ash, but you wanted my opinion.'

She hadn't. She'd wanted his agreement. 'Well what did you have in mind then?' She couldn't help the belligerent air creeping into her voice.

'Something laid back, simple I suppose.'

'Yes, that's all well and good, Quinn, but you're not giving me any examples, are you? I mean do we even bother having a head table or are you talking a picnic blanket on the fecking floor.' Her pitch had amped up several notches. 'Or, you know we could go the full hog and do a Pam Anderson, Tommy Lee job and wear our swimsuits and head off to the beach.'

'Bit cold, don't you think?' Quinn tried to make light of it. He didn't get where she was coming from. He was sure if she had longer to organise their nuptials, they'd be saying 'I do' in a castle and she'd have him in a purple suit like the one your man Becks wore on his big day. He'd seen the shiny photos thanks to his mammy having shoved the *Hello* magazine under his nose. She'd laughed and said if he wasn't careful his bride-to-be would have him decked out in similar gear and had he any thoughts on getting the highlights done because they looked ever so well in the photographs? No, he had not, he'd replied, failing to see the humour because it was all a bit too close to home. He risked a look at Aisling, she hadn't cracked a smile. 'Ash, don't you think you're getting a little carried away.'

Tony's chop, chop, chopping picked up pace and he kept his head down. Aisling wished he'd disappear and as the door burst open and Paula walked through her arms laden with dirty dishes, she wished she could click her fingers and make both her and Tony disappear. She didn't want the staff gossiping about her and Quinn. She took a deep breath.

'I'll get back to Leila and see if we can find something plainer.'

Quinn backtracked. 'No, don't do that. I want you to be happy with everything. It's grand so it is and sure, I'm a fella, what do we know about table settings and the like?'

The tightening in Aisling's chest eased as he offered her the olive branch. She took it.

'We'll find something in between,' she said, finally smiling. Quinn grinned back, pleased to have sidestepped an argument. Aisling made her excuses to leave saying she was needed back at the guesthouse and as she kissed him goodbye, she penned one of her letters to self.

Dear Aisling,

I'd like some advice please on the best way to tell my fiancé that the pumpkin shaped carriage I've my heart set on to take me to the church on our wedding day looks likely to be in the bag. I'm asking because he seems to have his heart set on a low-key day and there's nothing low key about a horse and carriage.

Yours faithfully,

Me

Chapter 7

Noreen

Noreen looked in the mirror of the fitting room. Shopping had been much more enjoyable when she was young. Mind there wasn't much money for shopping back then. Her mammy had made most of her clothes when she was a youngster and Noreen had been a dab hand with the sewing machine too. She'd even made her own wedding dress, repurposing the fabric from her mammy's gown into a modern style with a bolero jacket. Everybody had said she looked a picture. The old singer machine their dear mammy had sat hunched over until her eyes were no longer up to the task had gone to her. Rosamunde her younger sister had not objected but then she'd had a hard time putting so much as a pillow case together the year they'd done home economics! She conjured up an image of herself on her wedding day. The memory of how she'd nearly skipped up the aisle to stand next to her Malachy, so tall and handsome in his suit never failed to make her smile. How full of hopes and dreams for their future they'd been!

Life's not worth living if you don't have dreams when you're young Noreen often thought. She'd been heard to remark on occasion too that this was what was wrong with the youth of today. They had no oomph, no spark, worst of all no ambition. She'd seen spark in Rosamunde's daughter Emer's eyes from a young age and she'd found a kindred spirit in her niece. She'd felt back then, Emer would grow up to do great things and she closed her eyes for a moment remembering.

1961

'Here she is then.' Rosamunde pushed open the door to the shop, her oldest daughter Emer carrying her overnight bag by her side. 'Sure, you're a saint, Noreen.'

'Not at all.' Noreen straightened, her hand automatically going to the small of her back to ease the ache always lodged there from bending over. She'd been tidying the morning papers and the counter display while it was still quiet. 'Sure, I'm in need of someone to help me in the shop today what with Uncle Malachy away off to Galway for the races.' Malachy wasn't much of a betting man and she counted her blessing he wasn't a drinker like poor Bridie McAuley's husband, Tom, but he did like a flutter at the summer gee-gees and who was she to begrudge him that? 'Are you up to the job, Emer?'

'I am, Aunty Nono.' The little girl beamed at her. Emer had called her Aunty Nono when she was a tot and it had stuck. The two smiled at each other complicit in their understanding that no money would exchange hands but that Emer would be allowed to choose from an assortment of sweets to take upstairs later to munch on while her aunty carried on where they'd left off reading *The Water-Babies* the last time she'd stayed.

'Well, one less gives me a break, fives an odd number so it is. It's always four against one. Mammy told me to have another, even the number up or otherwise they'd be at each other day and night. She was right too.' She realised who she was babbling on to. 'Sorry, Noreen, that was thoughtless.'

'Ah, you're grand.' Noreen brushed the comment away although the casualness with which her younger sister spoke of having children stung. How many tears had she shed month after month since she got married? Rosamunde could be a tactless mare. Sure, she'd have been happy with one baby to bounce on her knee let alone five. Children though were a blessing the good Lord hadn't seen fit to bless her and Malachy with. It was something she'd grappled with and it had tested her faith but she was a good Catholic and, in the end, she'd listened to Father Michael who said God always had his reasons for doing what he did. He'd simply chosen a different path for her and Malachy, and it was up to her to steer them down it. She'd looked at things differently after that because her life was full of blessings. She had Malachy, they had their shop, and she made her mind up that God had bequeathed them the role of watching out for young Emer. It was a role she took seriously, very seriously indeed.

'Well,' Rosamunde said. 'I'd best be getting off home, I've a million and one done things to do and you know how useless Terry is. The last time I left him in charge on a Saturday, I got home and he'd tossed a sheet over the kitchen table and made it into a tent for the children. But, had he washed a dish or made a bed? No, he had not.'

Again, Noreen warded off the sting of her sister's words. Rosamunde didn't mean anything by it, she adored Terry as she adored her Malachy. He would have been the sort of dad who'd make a tent with a sheet over the kitchen table, too. She watched the way he was with Emer and it was bittersweet at times knowing he'd have made a grand daddy. She remembered herself. 'Here, Rosamunde, before you go, take one of these for the others.' She held out the jar with the lollipops and her sister smiled, 'You spoil them, Noreen, but I won't say no. One of them stuck in each of their gobs will give me some peace so it will.'

Her sister left and Noreen and Emer looked at each smiling. 'Now then, I've a box of tinned food needs putting away, do you think you can manage that, Emer?'

'I do, Aunty NoNo.'

'And then we'll have a bowl of soup and toast for lunch. How does that sound?'

'Grand, Aunty NoNo.'

Noreen's heart filled as she set the little girl her task and when Mrs Bunting bustled in wanting her order of bread and milk, she fussed over Emer exclaiming she was certain she'd grown this last while and wasn't she a good girl helping her aunt so.

Noreen had puffed up proud as she would have if Emer had been hers.

THE KNOCK ON THE FITTING room door, startled her back to the present and it took her a moment to reconcile the reflection in the mirror with the same woman who used to cherish those times with Emer forty years ago, now.

'How are you getting on, madam?' There was an edge of concern in the woman's voice and Noreen realised she'd been lost in her thoughts far longer than it should take to say yay or nay to a dress.

'I'm grand.'

'Is the size right, madam?'

'It is.'

'And does the jacket go well with it?'

'It does.'

'I'll leave you to it then, shall I?'

'Yes, please.'

Noreen smoothed the shiny royal blue fabric and sighed. She'd had a slim waist once, a girlish waist but look at her now. 'Put silk on a goat and it's still a goat,' she muttered deciding she might like the dress better in green. She wondered if the jacket the sales assistant had picked out came in green, too.

Chapter 8

Roisin followed her mammy through the car park, the sting of raindrops hitting her face despite her having pulled the hood of her coat up. The flight had been bumpy and she was feeling a little green around the gills.

'You'll be grand now you're back on solid ground, Rosi,' Maureen said, slowing her pace, 'So then, was your boss man alright about you having a Friday off?'

'He was, Mammy.'

'Will you be seeing Shay while you're here.'

'I hope so. It's not going to be easy finding time around everything Aisling's got planned.'

'Ah well, I'm sure you'll manage. And what's on Noah's agenda for the weekend?'

Roisin pulled a face. 'Colin will be taking him out and showing him the high life in London like he always does and Granny Quealey will be after filling him full of all his favourite foods. He'll have a grand time, so he will.'

'I'm still his number one nana though.' Maureen came to a screeching halt as she made a mental note to load Rosi up with her grandson's favourite sweets to take home with her. 'His Granny Quealey doesn't have a dog and Noah loves Pooh. Sure, he thought he was the best thing since sliced bread when I put him in charge of picking up his doings on our walks last time he was over.'

'He did, Mammy.' Roisin was pleased her son's fascination with the number two had waned. His latest predilection seemed to be trying to talk to Mr Nibbles like Doctor Doolittle could. She'd overheard him holding a conversation with him the other day that went along the lines of, 'Mr Nibbles, do you like lettuce or spinach better?' 'Lettuce. I don't blame you. Spinach makes me want to sick-up too.' She reassured her mammy, 'And of course, you're his number one.'

Satisfied, Maureen carried on toward the grey-storied car parking building. 'And do we ask how the gerbil is?'

'Mr Nibbles is thriving, Mammy. Apparently, he prefers the lettuce leaf to spinach and sure, this will make you laugh.' She relayed the tale of how Noah's beloved gerbil had performed another of his Houdini acts when he'd been staying overnight at the Quealey house. Colin's sour-faced mother had hit the roof when she found him nestled in the cup of her bra.

'What!' Maureen shrieked, envisaging all sorts of scenarios.

Roisin laughed, 'She wasn't wearing it at the time. It was on her bed and he decided her left cup made a lovely nest to hunker down in.

'Poor little thing, he lived to tell the tale obviously.'

'He did, but Colin wasn't popular with his mother. She said she felt violated and that the bra was her best Marks and Spencer's one and she'd had to bin it. She blames him for getting Noah Mr Nibbles in the first place. You know how I felt about him having a pet initially too, but I'm used to having him about the place now and I'd miss the sound of his mad scrabbling if he wasn't there.'

They reached the car and Roisin spied the eager poodle strapped into the front seat.

'You're in the back, Rosi.'

'But I feel sick and you know sitting in the back will only make it worse.'

'Rosi, don't be awkward. I can't drive with a howling dog in the back, now can I?' Maureen unlocked the car as Roisin opened the boot, lifting her case into it. She slammed it down mumbling something about a fecking dog coming before her eldest daughter as she ducked into the backseat. The poodle looked over the seat at her and she swore if she could talk to the animals like your man Doolittle, he'd have made a na-nana-naa-nah noise and stuck his paw to his nose to taunt her. She poked her tongue out at him.

'Have you said hello to Pooh, Rosi?' Maureen swivelled in her seat and Roisin knew they wouldn't be going anywhere until she'd given the dog a fuss. She sighed and petted the top of his head; he lapped up the attention.

'It's lovely to see our Rosi isn't it, Pooh? He's been ever such a good boy after the you know what.'

Roisin assumed she was talking about his having been neutered. Hopefully that meant the end of his amorous nose diving.

'Yes,' Maureen carried on, turning the key in the ignition. 'Rosemary Farrell's taken to calling in with a packet of doggy treats for him when she pops by. They're getting on great guns the pair of them these days, so they are.'

'Pleased to hear it,' Roisin said, folding her arms across her chest as her mammy reversed out of the parking space. Mammy's hair had kinked as Roisin's was prone to doing with the wet weather and she looked from Pooh and then back to her mammy. 'Did you know, Mammy, it is a scientific fact that people begin to resemble their dogs.'

Maureen swung around in her seat. 'I do not have facial hair, Roisin, thank you very much! If that's what you're getting at. It's the women on your father's side who all have the moustaches. It's very hard to hold a conversation with your great aunty Noreen because you wind up staring at it and the more you tell yourself not to the more you find yourself doing so. You'd want to watch out because it is a scientific fact, young lady, that the facial hair gene follows the father's side of the family.'

'You made that up, Mammy, and would you watch where you're going! We nearly hit that concrete bollard.'

Chapter 9

'What on earth is going on?' Roisin walked in through the door of O'Mara's dropping her suitcase down beside her as she surveyed the scene. She was still feeling nauseous from sitting in the back of the car and had spent the journey trying to focus on her breathing. She'd been tempted to get in Mammy's ear when they'd stopped at the lights and chant her childhood mantra of 'are we there yet' but as it happened she hadn't been able to get a word in which was annoying because she'd hoped she might be able, while they were on their own, to pump her for information about this mysterious man-friend of hers. She'd not said a word more since her New Year's Eve announcement and refused to be drawn on the topic. She was the proverbial closed book. Moira and Aisling had tried and now it was Roisin's turn. There'd been no chance though, Mammy had been full of the chat about the wedding and who the latest family member to announce they were coming was. Before she knew it, they were pulling up in front of the guesthouse.

Now Maureen, with a tight hold on the prancing Pooh, shut the door behind them as Roisin checked out Aisling. Her sister was red in the face and looked sweaty which an anomaly for the time of year. Come to that so was Bronagh. She frowned, noticing they were both dressed in their normal work attire yet Moira who didn't have so much as a bead of sweat on her forehead was posed at the foot of the stairs looking like she could possibly be the niece of Jane Fonda and was about to follow in her footsteps by making her own fitness video.

'How're ye, Rosi.' Aisling made to embrace her sister.

'Get off, wait until you've had a shower. What are you three up to?' She shot a look that conveyed the same sentiment to Bronagh.

'You've heard about our friendly little competition?' Moira asked, knowing full well she had because she'd written down Rosi's bet in her trusty notebook.

'I have.' Roisin wasn't owning up to who she was backing though. Bronagh could be fierce when she wanted to be. She surreptitiously looked from the two slimming competitors to see if either of them was looking a little less full in the face. Neither woman looked much different in her opinion.

'It's ridiculous. Two grown women competing to see who can lose weight the fastest,' Maureen tutted. She was backing Bronagh all the way despite her custard cream affliction or should that be addiction? Either way she knew Aisling inside and out. Her daughter took after her Nanna Dee and not just with her colouring. When she was under pressure, you'd be sure to find her with a gob full of something she'd helped herself to from the pantry. Nanna Dee had been exactly the same. 'I suggested they come along to line-dancing with myself and Rosemary Farrell. It's exercise that doesn't feel like exercise, Rosemary says. She loves it, so she does, although between us she's not very coordinated, always turning the wrong way and sticking the wrong leg out.' Maureen gave a demonstration of her new found line-dancing skills. 'I can do it better when I've got my boots on,' she said with a final clap of her hands.

'Since when did you like Country and Western, Mammy?' Roisin asked.

'I love Country and Western,' Maureen said. 'It always gets the toes a-tapping.'

'News to me.' Roisin shook her head. 'And what exactly are you doing, Moira?'

'Well,' Moira said, her hand resting on the bannister at the bottom of the stairs, a study of casualness in her active wear. 'Like I was saying before Mammy interrupted and gave us all her best Billy Ray Cyrus impersonation. I've decided to take on the role of personal trainer.'

'Good of you,' Roisin muttered, glancing at Bronagh and Aisling sympathetically.

It was Bronagh that piped up, 'She tried to make us pay her. Can you believe that?'

Roisin could quite believe it of her youngest sister. She took the opportunity to look at Bronagh's skirt. It was still straining across her middle but there was a possibility there weren't quite so many creases there as there'd been a month ago. She wondered if Moira might let her change her bet.

'And we told her to feck off,' Aisling added.

'Excuse me, ladies.' Moira tossed her ponytail indignantly, reminding Roisin of Black Beauty and she half expected her to whinny. She didn't but her voice did take on a braying timbre. 'This is my time.' She tapped her watch for effect. 'I could be in bed with a cup of tea and a plate of toast but I decided to get down these stairs and help you two along the road to weight loss success and do I get so much as thank you?' She looked to Roisin and her mammy expecting them to agree it was terribly ungrateful behaviour on Aisling and Bronagh's part. Roisin had already decided she wasn't getting caught in the middle and as for Maureen she gave Aisling a stingy flick on the backside as she caught sight of her giving her sister a rude finger sign.

'Don't you be doing things like that down here, Aisling. You know better than that. Sure, what would our guests think if they were to walk in and see their hostess giving them the finger.'

'I wasn't doing it at any of our guests, Mammy, and that hurt.'

'Yes, but they wouldn't know that would they?'

Roisin sighed she was home alright.

'Well, tell her to stop going on, Mammy,' Aisling whined.

'I'll bang both your heads together in a minute, so I will.'

'How's Pooh getting on, since his,' Bronagh mouthed the word, 'snip?'

'He's doing ever so well. Top of the class at puppy school. They all looked to where the puppy had a leg cocked threateningly over by the sofa.

'Pooh!' Maureen herded him out the door reappearing a moment later. 'It's alright,' she said. 'It was a number one, that's all. He's going through a phase of marking his territory. I think it's the trauma after the, you know what. He's feeling insecure.'

'Well you can't blame him now, can you?' Bronagh petted the dog. She was feeling a lot more affection for the fellow now he wasn't constantly trying to assault her. It was the wrong thing to do – there was life in the old dog (so to speak) yet it would seem. 'Get down, you naughty boy,' she shrieked.

'Right,' Roisin interjected. 'I want to get this case upstairs because as lovely as it is standing about in reception listening to you lot carrying on, I've a phone call to make before we head off to the bridal shop.'

'Lover boy?' Moira asked, blocking the stairs.

'If you mean Shay, then yes. He knows this weekend is all about Aisling and the wedding but I'm sure we can manage to squeeze in a catch-up. Maybe tonight; there's not much planned this evening is there, Ash?'

Aisling shook her head.

'It's not a catch-up you're after, it's a ride,' Moira said. 'A gallop around the track with your stallion,' she added lewdly.

'Moira O'Mara, have you forgotten your mammy is standing right here.'

Silence fell as a thought occurred to all three sisters simultaneously. Their eyes swung to their mammy. Could she be...? *Nooo!* they silently screamed. That would be wrong on so many counts. Moira decided to change the subject, still not allowing Roisin to pass.

'Mammy, you're not wearing those out, are you? Sure, you've worn the material across the arse so thin I can tell you what colour your knickers are. Wedding boutiques are posh places not geriatric strip joints.'

Maureen glanced down at the yoga pants she'd commandeered off Roisin the last time she'd come to stay. They were her favourites, her trusty go-tos for comfort and ability to bend, stride and lunge. Her eyes darted toward Roisin's case and she wondered if she'd packed any more. She'd try her luck later. Now though, she had a mouthy daughter to contend with. 'It's called common sense, Moira. They're very easy to whip on and off for trying outfits on, thank you, and your posh wedding shop woman won't giving a flying fig what any of us are wearing so long as we splash the cash.'

Aisling thought Mammy had a point there. The bridal shop woman, she'd gleaned from her dealings with her over the telephone, was a bit of a fecky brown noser type, she'd get on well with Patrick.

'And for your information, madam, you couldn't possibly know what colour my underpants are, because I am wearing the thing.'

Aisling frowned her mind beginning to boggle. 'What thing?'

'You know, the thing. The thing you girls all get about with.'

Her three daughters shook their heads with no clue as to what she was on about.

'The thing, the string thing that goes up your—'

'Jaysus wept, Mammy, the thong,' Moira cringed. 'Too much information!'

Roisin went pale, wondering if there was a reason her mammy had stopped wearing the underpants that came up to her chin.

Aisling, aghast, said, 'No, Mammy, it's my day and I don't want to see your arse every time I step into the changing room. You're to put some sensible knickers on before we go.'

The bickering carried on all the way up the stairs to the family apartment.

Chapter 10

Madame Mullan with her gleaming blonde chignon and exquisitely cut yellow silk wrap dress was like a golden vision and Aisling had whispered this sentiment to Moira moments after they'd arrived at the Bridal Emporium. They'd received the sort of welcome reserved for royalty or Westlife as they piled boisterously in the door of the boutique but as their feet sank into the luxuriously thick pile carpet and they'd taken in their surrounds, they'd quietened down. The Bridal Emporium was the type of establishment where it felt appropriate to whisper reverently, a bit like being in church. Moira had whispered back that Madame Mullan reminded her of a giant dandelion but in a good way. Aisling wasn't sure what to make of that comment but she'd begun to feel a tad nervous at Madame's effusiveness. She was, after all, a shopkeeper, albeit a golden one, and shopkeepers were only ever *that* nice to people they thought were going to spend loads of money.

Mammy was giving her and Quinn a very generous contribution toward the wedding but even so, this place reeked of the green stuff in a way that was making her tummy jump about. Especially with Quinn making noises about house buying and the like. And was that a runway? There was a raised platform with curtains leading into the fitting rooms from which, she presumed she'd emerge. A cluster of seats were arranged in front of the stage for the bridal party to pass verdict. Aisling sniffed, detecting the hint of a floral fragrance floating on the

air. Chanel No. 5 perhaps? She shook the nerves aside; she'd
come this far, now was not the time to worry about her finances. She sniffed again, wondering what the odds were of
Madame Mullan using the same air freshener Mammy had
been doing the hard sell on lately. Anyone would think she was
getting a backhander from the company the way she went on
about it. Moira elbowed her. 'Don't do that.'

'What?'

'That sniffy thing you're after doing, it makes you look like
a gingery seal coming up for air.'

She ignored Moira as she pondered whether she'd made
a mistake coming here. She caught sight of her face, pale and
slightly drawn, in the reflection of one of the freestanding gilt
framed mirrors that seemed to be dotted about the place. They
were all set to a flattering angle but still, she wished she hadn't.
Maybe she should have gotten over herself and gone back to
Ivory Bridal Couture; at least she knew what to expect there. It
didn't feel right though not after last time. It would be a bit like
rendezvousing with her ex. She glanced nervously at Leila who
smiled back at her reassuringly and she felt a little better until
Moira broke rank and made a beeline for a rack of shimmering
sheaths.

'Oh, Aisling, this is gorgeous, so it is, look,' she held the
wisps of soft lilac fabric up against her and had a delirious look
on her face that said she was imagining herself on the red carpet, about to give her Oscars' night speech, or something like.

It was also microscopic, Aisling noted with alarm. Well not
quite, but in Aisling's experience the less fabric the more expensive it was likely to be. An internal tug-o-war ensued. She wanted to march over and inspect the price tag but at the same time

she didn't want Madame Mullan over there to think she was a penniless hick. She was still wrestling with herself as Moira whipped the same dress in pink and baby blue off the rack and trotted off toward the dressing room. Happy as a pig in muck.

Leila whispered in her ear, 'Discourage her, no matter how gorgeous she looks. You need to keep three things in mind. Price tag, headlights and Uncle Colm. Alright? Remember this is a winter wedding not a Maldives getaway.'

Aisling nodded obediently.

'Come on, let's check out the wedding gowns.' Leila pulled her toward the headless mannequins posed in a group of three, all draped in sumptuous silks. 'Oh, these are stunning, Ash,' she said, pausing in front of a sophisticated ivory dress that had Aisling sighing wistfully. She'd never get away with that, not with her thighs. Leila however put it more tactfully. 'Ivory's not your colour. We need diamond white or champagne would be lovely. Have you a particular style in mind?'

They both looked at the row of dresses spanning the length of the emporium. The opposite wall was devoted to the brides-maids and the back wall catered to the mother of the bride. Aisling hadn't a clue where to start and was grateful she had her friend here to help her. 'I suppose I'd like a mermaid trumpet-style dress with lace, lots of lace.' She wondered why Leila was staring at her sympathetically and then it dawned on her. She'd described the dress she'd chosen the last time. She pressed her lips together in a grim line. 'What I should have said was I want the exact opposite of a lacy mermaid trumpet dress.'

Before they could even begin their search however, Moira poked her head through the curtains, about to be the first to strut the catwalk as she demanded everybody stop what they were doing. When she was certain she had everyone's attention she flung the curtains open and struck a hands on hip pose, one shapely leg thrust out of a split between the lilac wisps as though she had indeed stopped for a photo call on the red carpet.

Madame Mullan was a bee to honey as she took the two steps to the platform and homed in on Moira to begin adjusting the straps and pinching the dress in at the waist before looking toward Aisling expectantly.

'It's lovely, and you look a picture, Moira. But don't you think you might be a little cold on the day and that material is awfully sheer. It's going to be February after all. Madame Mullan do you have anything with long sleeves you could show Moira? In a more, erm, substantial fabric perhaps.'

Moira scowled at her sister, 'Should we wear our flannelette nighties and be done with it,' she muttered, stomping back into the fitting room while Madame Mullan fluttered off, a golden butterfly gone in search of bridesmaids' dresses in a more appropriate style.

Leila patted Aisling on the back. 'Well done you.'

Aisling mustered up a smile and began to sift through the heavy dresses on the rack. They were beautiful, all of them, but some were too fussy, some too simple. The perfect dress had yet to put in an appearance.

'Ash, what do you think of this one?' Leila asked, breaking her price tag first rule.

Aisling's breath caught at the sight of the dress her friend was holding up with some difficulty for her to see. 'It's like something from a fairy tale.'

'Fabulous isn't it? It makes me wish I was getting married so I could wear it. Look at the way it ties at the back here. Oh, I can so see you in this, Aisling.' The note of excitement in Leila's voice was catching and Aisling reached out to touch the neckline above the bodice gently.

'Are those crystals do you think?' she asked, admiring the way the light was catching them.

'They're Swarovski crystals, all hand sewn on. A divine gown. I can see you're both women of exquisite taste.' Madame Mullan had floated over to catch the tail end of their conversation. 'Shall I put it in the dressing room for you to try.'

Yes, she was a definite fecky brown noser, Aisling thought, looking at Leila who was nodding emphatically.

'You definitely want to try.'

Aisling didn't want to ruin the moment by asking how much it cost so she trailed behind Madame Mullan, nearly bumping into Moira who was dressed in her civvies once more as she exited the fitting room. 'I've several dresses for you to look at, as soon as I've hung this in the dressing room for our bride-to-be, here,' Madam Mullan directed at her and Moira nodded, more interested in the gown she had over her arm. 'Wow! That's gorgeous. What colour do you call that?'

'It's champagne,' Madame Mullan said. 'The perfect choice for madam's delicate colouring.'

'Can't wait to see you in it, Aisling.'

Aisling felt a spark of excitement at her younger sister's unusually generous words. It was a gorgeous, fabulous fairy tale dress and she couldn't wait to step into it. A little voice spoke up. She suspected it belonged to her conscience because it was telling her if she were going to be buying a house in the foreseeable future then she should check out the price before going any further. There was no point falling in love with the gown and then not being able to justify the price. She hesitated but only briefly before telling her conscience to feck off away with itself as she traipsed on into the fitting room.

A moment later Aisling found herself alone with the dress which Madame Mullan had hung up telling her she'd be back to assist her with the grand reveal in ten minutes. She fluffed off to show Moira, Roisin and Leila her suggestions in the bridesmaid department. Aisling gazed around the spacious fitting room, breathing in the subtle fragrance of flowers clinging to the air thanks to the aromatherapy diffuser on the occasional table. A pile of wedding magazines and a box of tissues were artfully arranged next to it and in the corner was a white Queen Anne styled chair with a plush red velvet seat. She clambered out of her trousers and was pleased the lighting was subtle. Otherwise she'd have been gasping at the sight of her flesh in all its bare, fluorescent glory reflected back at her, thanks to the floor to ceiling mirrors. Her sweater was halfway over her head when Mammy's voice echoed around the room.

'Holy God above tonight, Aisling, could you not have put underwear on!'

Aisling pulled the sweater off feeling her hair frizz out from the static. 'Mammy, don't shout and what are you on about? I have a bra and knickers on. Sensible, suitable ones too.'

Maureen's hand rested on her chest and her expression was one of relief as she got nearer. 'Jesus, Mary and Joseph thank God you do. It's the colour. I couldn't see it when I walked in. You gave me a terrible fright, so you did. You girls don't normally wear beige undergarments.'

'They're not beige thank you very much, Mammy, the colour is nude.' Jaysus, Mammy could be an ignoramus; as if she'd ever wear beige anything, Aisling was outraged at the very thought. 'And I chose it so my bra straps wouldn't be glaringly obvious when I tried the dresses on.'

'Yes, well nude is exactly what I thought you were.'

Aisling shook her head and mumbled, 'Give me strength,' before moving toward the dress.

'I've come to help you get into that. Moira's got your Madame one running around like a headless chicken.' She looked to where the dress was shimmering under the lights and her gasp was audible.

'Aisling, oh my word.' The hand went to the chest once more. 'It's beautiful, so it is.'

'It is, isn't it? Leila spotted it.'

'I can't wait to see you in it,' She echoed Moira's sentiment. 'Come on.' Maureen was pleased to feel useful as she carefully removed the dress from the hanger and helped her daughter into it. 'Alright now then, let's zip you up. Raise your arms.'

'Go slowly, don't pinch me.' Aisling said as her mammy began to inch the zipper up.

'That only happened the once, Aisling.'

Once was more than enough, Aisling thought wincing at the memory of the formal dress she'd insisted on squeezing into for her high school leavers dance.

'Alright so. We're a quarter of the way there, on the count of three it's time to breathe in. Alright?'

Aisling nodded assent.

'One, two, three.'

She sucked everything in with all her might but still Maureen could only get the zip halfway up. 'I don't want to force it, Aisling, and breathe out or you'll be after fainting. I'm sure it can be let out a little.'

'It won't need to be. I'm on track to have lost five pounds by D-Day.'

Maureen stepped away from her daughter in order to give her a head to toe once over. Her hands formed a steeple which she held to her mouth and she began blinking rapidly.

'Mammy, you're not going to cry, are you?'

'Not at all.' Her voice wavered in a manner that said that's exactly what she was about to do.

Aisling looked at her reflection and a smile began to form on her lips as she felt her anxiety unknot itself and float away. How could anything go wrong on her wedding day if she looked like this? Sure, she felt like a princess.

'Mammy, I love it' Her voice was quiet as she took in the sheer long sleeves and high neckline iridescent with crystals. The bodice beneath was corset styled and she held her hair up and looked in the mirror behind her so she could see the pearl beading which began at the top of the corset ribbons and finished at her neck. The heavy sateen fabric of the skirt had a lace overlay and it flowed from the waist without being full. She turned this way and that, not quite believing it was her looking back at her in the mirror.

'Aisling O'Mara, you are perfect.' Maureen sniffled, reaching for a tissue from the box on the occasional table and giving her nose an almighty blow.

Madame Mullan announced her presence, her eyes lighting up at the sight of Aisling as she made all the right noises before titivating with the fabric. Maureen was sniffling away and Madame Mullan passed her the box of tissues, well used to tearful mammies. 'Why don't you go and join the rest of the bridal party and ask them to take a seat?

Maureen gave a final sniff before doing as she was asked.

'Are you ready?'

Aisling's stomach fluttered at the thought of showing her sisters and Leila her dress and she nodded as Madame Mullan arranged her in front of the curtains before pulling the cord and opening them.

She was suddenly vulnerable as she stood under the lights. Would her sisters and best friend see what she and Mammy had seen or would they think the dress ostentatious? She knew she could count on Moira for an honest opinion. She smiled tremulously looking from one to the other. Delight and admiration was mirrored back at her and her worries settled as she enjoyed her moment in the sun. Roisin joined her mammy with the sniffling, Leila clapped her hands together and Moira got up and jumped on stage throwing her arms around her sister as she said, 'You look amazing, Ash.' It was all the confirmation she needed.

Chapter 11

Aisling sipped her champagne enjoying the sparkly, seductive flavour that was making her feel even more giddy than she already did. It was a lovely touch on Leila's part, the cracking open of a bottle of Moet to celebrate her having chosen her dress. She'd arranged the glasses to be on hand prior to the appointment with Madame Mullan who'd declined a glass even though she should be celebrating given how much Aisling was going to be spending this afternoon. Leila had even thought to bring a bottle of bubbly grape juice for Moira, a gesture which made her want to hug her, so she did. 'You're the best wedding planner in the world,' she'd gushed as Moira popped the cork on her fizz.

Now her gaze flitted to where her dress was hanging on the rack beside the counter awaiting the equivalent of a down payment on a house before she'd be allowed to take it home where it belonged. The sensible part of her brain, the part that told her nobody needed to spend that much on a dress decided to put in an appearance. But then she recalled how the dress had made her feel. It truly was a Cinderella dress and what sum did you put on a gown that made you feel like you were the star of your very own fairy story?

Would Quinn buy into her fairy tale dream or would he see pound signs when he saw her in the dress. Perhaps when she told him they were saving on the shoes he'd come around to what it cost. He could be quite thrifty when he wanted to be could Quinn. To appease him she'd wear the Prada satin pumps she'd tucked away from her first attempt at getting married. They would go perfectly and she held no fear of being jinxed where shoes were concerned, besides which, she knew she'd be hard pressed to find another pair she loved as much. So, it wasn't much of a compromise at all on her part to roll with the shoes she already had but Quinn didn't need to know that. Come to that there was no need for him to know how much this dress and the bridesmaids' dresses, once decided upon, were setting her back. Men hadn't a clue when it came to things like that anyway. Again, she ignored the niggle that given they were about to share the rest of their life together he should be privy to how much the wedding was costing them but, it wasn't as if he'd asked. When she had tried to broach things with him his eyes had glazed over as if she were doing a long and involved maths equation.

She'd been reluctant to climb out of the dress; she'd have liked to have stayed in it forever and if she'd had her way, she'd have worn it home. She'd pictured herself riding on the top of the double decker bus as it rumbled through the streets of Dublin, waving to all and sundry. But then she'd seen it was still raining outside and had changed the fantasy to her sitting in the back of a taxi with tinted windows. The windows had to be tinted because people always wondered who was behind them. She could roll them down when they were stopped at the lights and give the peasants, whoops, pedestrians, going about their normal working day a wave. Gosh, the champers was going to her head, she thought, eyeing the flute glass, knowing her cheeks had flushed pink.

That the dress was meant for her was a given. Madame Mullan had seized the sales opportunity gushing about how rare it was to find the perfect gown so quickly. Aisling fancied she could see the dollar signs in her eyes and hear her brain making a *ker-ching* sound. She'd only been brave enough to look at the price tag once she'd taken the precious dress off and had nearly fallen over at all the zeros. There was no going back though and a song had sprung to mind, Sinead O'Connor's *Nothing Compares to You*. It was now stuck in her head.

She downed what was left in her glass and dragged her eyes away from the dress. She might be sorted but nobody else was and time was a-ticking. 'Right, ladies,' she said, 'what have you found?' It was directed at her bridesmaids.

Moira was the first to hold a dress up. It was midnight blue with ruching around the waist and bell sleeves. 'I love this.'

'It's gorgeous, but does it come in a different colour. Midnight blue's not Leila's colour.' It would wash her out Aisling thought.

They all looked expectantly at Madame Mullan who shook her head with an expression that could have been about to convey the most tragic of news. 'No, it is a one-off and as such only in the blue.'

'A one-off,' Moira said, clearly liking the idea as she stroked the silky fabric. 'And I look very well in blue, so I do.'

'Moira you'd look grand in a sack and remember who's paying,' Aisling said.

Moira put the dress back.

'What about this?' Roisin pulled a gown from the rack and showed them it. She'd checked the price and it wasn't exorbitant although she hadn't worked out the times three. It was very generous of Aisling to fork out for her, Leila and Moira's dresses and she was grateful given her current financial situation. Thanks to her feckless ex-husband there wouldn't be much of a financial settlement once the divorce was finalised and with the cost of living in London, she had to watch every penny. Unlike Moira, however, she didn't want to send her sister to the poor house.

'Oh, I like that!' Leila exclaimed. Moira mooched over and gave a grunt that signalled she thought it was alright but wasn't ready to relinquish her blue dress yet.

'Mammy? What do you think?' Aisling asked. She was feeling magnanimous toward her mammy after her effusive gushing over the dress, that and the champers.

Maureen came over and stroked the maroon silk fabric. 'It's a wrap style which is very flattering so it is and none of you'd have to worry about the sucky-in knickers but I'm not sure about the colour. It would be grand on Moira and Rosi but it's on the dark side for Leila.'

'What about this, ladies.' Madame Mullan produced, seemingly from thin air, a blush velvet drop waist dress. 'And I happen to have it in each of your sizes.'

'Oh, I like that,' Maureen gushed. 'You won't catch your death in it either. Sure, you could almost get away with a spencer underneath it.'

Leila bit back her smile at the look of horror on Moira's face the mention of a spencer had invoked. 'Maureen's spoken, ladies, looks like we're trying the velvet number on,' she said.

'This one is perfect for you, mademoiselle.' Madame handed the dress to Leila. 'I shall fetch the other two from out the back,' Madame Mullan said, gliding off with the sort of speed that had Aisling checking to see if it were roller skates and not shoes on her feet. Roisin, Leila and Moira took themselves off to the fitting room to wait, leaving Maureen and Aisling alone.

'Mammy, have you seen anything you like?'

'I haven't had a chance to look yet, Aisling. I was keeping an eye on Moira for you. She's not got an ounce of common sense in that head of hers at times. It's a winter wedding but she'd be following you down the aisle in a floaty sundress if it was up to her.'

Aisling agreed with her. It was hard trying to keep everyone happy but she had her fingers crossed for the blush pink numbers. Officially, Roisin was supposed to be helping Mammy with her outfit. Aisling had put her in charge of supervising her. She'd told her big sister in no uncertain terms that Mammy wasn't to be so much as sniffing in the direction of anything silky and red. There'd be no China Beach, prostitute style dresses at her wedding, she'd declared out of earshot of Mammy while they'd sheltered from the rain under a shop awning, waiting for the bus to bring them here to the Bridal Emporium.

It wasn't working out like that though and it looked like she was going to be the one overseeing what she picked out. Maybe it wasn't such a bad thing. Roisin could have been looking for payback for the crochet toilet dolly wedding dress Mammy had talked her into wearing on her big day. 'Shall we see if anything jumps out at you then?' she asked, steering her over to the mother of the bride section. 'It would be grand if we all went home with our dresses today. I could cross that off my list then.' The handwritten list of things to organise between now and February 14 seemed never ending, even with Leila's services, because it was still up to her, to yay or nay everything and Quinn wasn't much cop.

'Would you like any assistance?' Madame Mullan simpered, with two more of the velvet dresses draped over her arm. 'I won't be a moment.'

'No, thank you, but if you could keep an eye on them in there, that would be grand.' Aisling inclined her head toward the fitting room from where fits of giggles were emanating.

'Certainly, madam.' She disappeared off in that direction and Aisling and Maureen began to mill around the mother of the bride section. The outfits on the mannequins didn't grab either of them.

'Dowdy, so they are,' Maureen declared. 'Have you seen Quinn's mam's outfit?'

'I don't think Mrs Moran's bought anything yet.'

Maureen frowned, she'd have liked a heads-up as to what the competition was wearing.

'How's she doing these days?'

'Grand, she's doing grand.' Quinn's mam had suffered a stroke the previous year but had battled her way through to recovery, although she got tired very quickly these days. Aisling explained this to her mammy. 'It's why she didn't come with us today. She didn't want to slow us down. I wouldn't have minded though.'

'It's a shame she didn't come. I'd have liked the opportunity to get to know her better. I must invite her to lunch now that we're going to be family. What will you call her?'

'What do you mean?' Aisling asked.

'Well you can hardly call her Mrs Moran after you're married, now can you? And you already have a mammy.' She pointed to her chest. 'Me.'

'I know that, thank you, and one mammy is plenty.'

'Well then, what's it going to be?'

'I'll probably call her Maeve. She keeps asking me to.' It didn't roll easily off Aisling's tongue, she'd always been Mrs Moran to her.

'That's very forward, Aisling. I didn't raise you to call your elders by their first names. Sure, do you not remember that precocious little madam from your playgroup who called her mammy, Dervla? It was all Dervla this and Dervla that. It didn't sound right coming from a child and if she'd tried it on me, I'd have sorted her out.'

'No, I don't remember, Mammy, but then I'd have only been three at the time. And I don't see the point of your story anyway, given the difference between a little girl calling her mammy by her first name and a woman in her mid-thirties addressing her mammy-in-law by her first name.'

Maureen made the face she always made when she didn't want to admit she could be wrong, but she was saved from having to say anything by the sudden sound of Madame Mullan's excited voice.

'Oh, éclatant!' she exclaimed from the fitting room.

Mammy and Aisling looked at one another although neither had a clue as to what she'd said.

'She's not French you know. I think she's from Tipperary. Listen closely, it's in the way she rolls her r's and McBride is about as French as—'

'My arse,' Aisling finished for her and Maureen nodded her agreement. They giggled, co-conspirators.

'It might be nice for your outfit to coordinate with the bridesmaids' dresses.' Aisling said moving toward the more subtle colours on the rack.

Maureen nodded thoughtfully but said, 'I like the bold colours more myself.' She homed in on a red two-piece suit. Aisling grimaced behind her back, the warm champagne fuzz wearing off at the sight of it. She knew her mammy well enough though to be tactful or she'd dig her heels in and the red outfit would be the one going home with them, purely because she didn't like being told what to do. Where Mammy was concerned, she considered it her job to be telling everyone else what *they* should be doing.

'Ah but, Mammy,' Aisling cast about quickly and whipped the first item off the rack that came to hand. Distraction was key. 'Look at this.' She waved it under her nose. 'Sure, you'd look like a million dollars in this. Oh yes, you'd look like you'd stepped out of the pages of *Hello*.' She knew Mammy scoured the magazine's shiny pages each time she went to the hairdressers.

Maureen paused and took stock of the dress Aisling was shaking about. 'Hold still for a minute would you so I can get a better look. It was simple and elegant which a woman of her height and bust size needed in order not to look fussy. She stopped stroking the red suit and moved toward the champagne coloured, fitted dress. She liked the lacy sleeves. 'Sure, it's the same colour as your wedding gown.'

Aisling looked at it properly and liked what she saw. It was elegant and classy. Not words that sprang to mind when she thought of her mammy but there was a first time for everything. She sensed she could be on to a winner if she played her cards right. 'Mammy,' she encouraged. 'The photographs would look ever so stylish with us all coordinated like and you could go big with your hat. It's a dress that needs a big hat.'

'A big hat, you say?' Maureen envisaged herself in all her champagne-matching-dress glory peeping out from under the brim of a large hat which was dipping down over one eye to give her an air of the mysterious mammy of the bride. She was sold. 'I'll try it on.'

Aisling did a mental happy dance. The icing on the cake came a moment later when Moira appeared from between the fitting room curtains, 'Are you watching.'

'Yes,' Aisling and Maureen turned their attention to the platform. The curtains opened and Moira danced her way out in front of them looking pretty in pink. She was seemingly happy with her dress as she began to sing, *Girl's Just Want to Have Fun*. Leila and Roisin were on backing.

Chapter 12

Noreen

N oreen's feet were aching from the day's shopping and it was a relief to board the bus that would take her home to Claredoncally. She was always glad to see the back of the city and return to her village where people were civilised and still managed to say good morning and good afternoon to one another. Manners cost nothing but they'd been in short supply on the town's streets today. Sure, look at the driver, he'd barely acknowledged her as she'd presented her senior's card to him. Still, at least it had been a successful day's shopping and she wasn't going home empty handed, she thought, bustling her way down the aisle. She had to be careful not to knock the bag containing her new hat or the bubble wrapped and boxed Waterford crystal vase she'd chosen as a wedding gift for Aisling and whatever his name was. Her lips curved at the bargain she'd gotten.

She picked a seat halfway down the bus then immediately wished she hadn't as the woman in front of her reeked of perfume. Noreen wouldn't have been surprised if she'd been in Boots having free squirts of whatever was on offer because the smell was an eyewatering and confusing mix of flowers and spices. She shuffled across her seat so she was next to the window and placed her bags down on the aisle seat. It was done in the hope of warding anyone off who was of a mind to sit down next to her and while away the hour-long journey by chattering because she was too weary for small talk.

She glanced at the Debenham's bag on the seat beside her. Noreen missed Roches Stores where the service had been second to none but she'd done alright in its replacement department store. The sales assistant had carefully folded and wrapped her dress, with the matching jacket she'd managed to find, in tissue paper which she hoped would be enough to prevent it taking on the scent of whatever that woman in front of her had tipped all over herself. She'd gone for the green in the end because Malachy had always liked her in green.

Of course, once she'd solved the problem of what she was going to wear to Aisling's wedding, she'd had to think about shoes, handbag and a hat. There was no point letting the dress down with mismatched accessories. Speaking of shoes, her ankles felt like they were spilling over the top of hers. Fluid retention Doctor Finnegan had said when she'd been to see him about it. It happened when she'd been on her feet too long. She'd soak them in Epsom salts tonight.

A young lad slouched past her and she tsked silently. No oomph in him, no get up and go, and he could do with pulling his trousers up, too. A slovenly appearance made for a slovenly mind in her opinion. Not that she'd tell him this; she'd probably get a mouthful for her efforts because these young ones had no respect for their elders. She was wishing they could get on their way when the bus rumbled into life, slowly pulling out into the afternoon traffic. It was nearly time for the children to be getting out of school and their mammies would all be roaring off to pick them up. When did children stop walking to school? she wondered. It was no wonder this generation were a pack of lazy so-and-sos, not willing to work hard to get to where they wanted to be in life. Emer had tried to take short-cuts too and look where it had gotten her.

The urban scenery gave way to the rocky, rugged landscape of her beloved County Cork. As she spied a rainbow stretching boldly over the fields, Noreen began to breathe easier now there was distance between herself and the city. She was in two minds about her upcoming visit to Dublin. The pace of the place terrified her but it would be nice to have a weekend of being waited on at O'Mara's and to see the family. Maureen had told her when she'd rung to confirm she was coming that it looked likely Cormac would be over from America. He'd be giving Aisling away in place of her daddy. Sad business that was, Brian getting the cancer she thought. It would be good to see Cormac again though. It had been far too long between visits. She'd always had a soft spot for him although she'd never un-derstood why he'd upped and left and gone all that way to boot. He'd never married either which was a shame because he had a lovely nature as a young lad, very gentle. He'd have made some lucky lass a grand husband. It was a waste was what it was.

Her mind flitted back to Emer as the bus stopped to let the scraggly bunch of sheep, who'd decided they had the right of way, mosey across to the opposite field. What would she look like now? She didn't like to think about the last time she'd laid eyes on her. Words had been said that had sliced like a knife through the bond between them. Emer had been eigh-teen years old. She'd be in her late forties now or was she fifty? Noreen was too tired to do the sums. Rosamunde had tele-phoned not long after Aisling's wedding invitation had arrived. She'd said it was an opportunity to mend bridges as Emer had accepted the invite and would Noreen see her way to patching things up with her? Sure, Rosamunde had said, it was years ago and it did no one any good to hold onto grudges. What Rosamunde didn't understand, Noreen thought listening to her, was that it wasn't a grudge she held. No, not at all. It was a wound she carried with her. A wound that, even now, hurt when it was being prodded like it was being prodded by this wedding.

The bus juddered forth and the fields outside, as the rainbow had done moments earlier, faded into the background her mind spinning backwards.

1966

'Oh, Aunty Nono, Uncle Malachy! It's gorgeous, so it is.' Emer with a party hat perched precariously on top of her dark head held the sterling silver cross pendant up to the light. Her dark brown eyes were shining. The jeweller's box along with the birthday card they'd chosen for her were open on the table in front of the place they all thought of as hers at the table.

Noreen and Malachy exchanged pleased glances with one another. They'd made a special trip into town to Longford's the Jewellers last Friday having got young Seamus, who helped out after school with the deliveries, to man the fort for them. Off they'd tootled in their little white van that Malachy used to collect the fresh produce from the markets over in Culdoon. Noreen never had learned to drive. She'd sat enjoying the ride with her handbag perched on her knee, feeling very smart in her new green, boiled wool coat and matching hat.

Longford's was the same jewellery shop from where they'd bought their wedding bands all those years ago and Noreen had been nostalgic as she stepped over the threshold, the memories of their younger selves washing over her. Mr Longford Senior had retired but his son had taken over the family business. He was the spit of his father which was rather unnerving because it had made Noreen feel as though time had stood still inside the doors of store until she'd caught sight of her and Malachy in the reflection of the glass cabinet. Mr Longford Junior had been happy to show them his range of necklaces, in particular those suitable for a young lady.

It had been Malachy's idea to get Emer a pendant. He wanted her to have something she could keep. Sixteen was an awkward age from memory, he'd said, turning the open sign to closed on the door of their convenience store a fortnight before. It would be nice to get her something that made her feel like a young lady and what did Noreen think to a necklace of some sort. Noreen had been proud of her husband. He was such a wonderfully, thoughtful man.

They'd spent an age pouring over the tray in Longford's wanting to get it right because sixteen was an awkward age in more ways than one, and girls these days knew what they liked.

Malachy had something in mind that wouldn't snap if Emer forgot to take it off when she was sleeping; she tended on the forgetful side he explained to Mr Longford, who told them he knew exactly the sort of thing they were after. He was the father of three girls himself he'd informed them, steering them toward a chain that while strong was not chunky. The cross they decided on was small and delicate. Emer would wear it not the other way around which was as it should be, Noreen thought. She didn't like ostentatious jewellery. Malachy had looked to her and she'd nodded that yes, the chain and the cross were just right. The pendant was placed with satisfying finesse into a pale lavender box with a silk lining and Noreen was sure Mr Longford's ears had twitched as she turned to Malachy and said, 'You know we'll have to do the same for the others when they turn sixteen don't you. We can't be seen to have favourites.' Malachy had agreed with her. It didn't need to be said that while they couldn't be *seen* to have a favourite niece or nephew it didn't mean they didn't have one.

There was a spring in both their steps as Mr Longford saw them to the door. It was at the thought of young Emer's face when she opened this special gift safely tucked inside Noreen's handbag.

'Shall we have a fish and chip supper?' Malachy had suggested as Noreen linked her arm through his and, even though it wasn't Friday and they never ate fish on any day except Friday, Noreen said that was a grand idea indeed and very nice it had been too.

Emer, Noreen saw now, was undoing the clasp. She got up from her seat. 'Here I'll help you with that. Pass me my glasses, Malachy.' He did so and she slid them on to the end of her nose instructing her niece. 'Hold your hair up, Emer.' She placed the chain around her neck and, peering through the bottom of her lens, secured it. 'There we are. Now then, let's have a look at you.'

Emer's thick waves fell back down around her shoulders and she swivelled in her seat to show her aunty the necklace.

'Sure, you look a picture, Emer,' Noreen said, feeling the smarting of tears in her eyes as she gazed at her nearly grown-up niece. Her heart swelled at what a beautiful young woman she was becoming. Malachy too, made an approving noise and Emer got up, eager to see her gift for herself. 'I'm going to have a look in the bathroom mirror.'

Noreen waited for her niece to disappear and then, winking at Malachy, she went into the kitchen to retrieve the Victoria sponge she'd laboured over. How pleased she'd been to see a deep cake emerge from the oven which sprang back when pressed as it should do. The airy sponge was filled with fresh cream and she shook the icing sugar on top, the finishing touch. She wouldn't bother with candles. They'd already had a birthday celebration at Rosamunde and Terry's with the younger children all squealing with delight over the chocolate cake their mammy had made. It wasn't long before their faces were covered in buttercream and the floor littered with crumbs as with mouths stuffed full of cake, they begged their sister to open her presents.

Emer had been keen to come back with her aunty and uncle to stay the night because she was going to catch the bus to town to go to the cinema with her friends as a birthday treat in the morning. The shop was only five-minute's walk from where the bus stopped. Noreen had been unable to resist making the sponge even though none of them needed any more cake. As she carried it out to the table, Malachy, with his sweet tooth, sat up a little straighter in his chair at the prospect of two slices of cake in one day and Emer who'd re-joined her uncle at the table clapped her hands.

'You spoil me, Aunty Nono!' She beamed up at her, her cheeks rosy with pleasure at all the attention. Noreen put the cake down and sliced a fat wedge for the birthday girl. She knew she spoiled her but she was worth the spoiling and sure, it wasn't like they had anyone else to fuss around.

Chapter 13

Aisling looked in the mirror as Tara, whose own hair was cut in a symmetrical jet-black bob a la Uma Thurman, *Pulp Fiction,* pulled her hair back from her shoulders. 'Did you bring in any pictures of what you had in mind, Aisling?' Her gravelly voice suggested she spent a lot of time standing around out the back of the salon on cigarette breaks. She had an incredible number of piercings too, which were making Aisling wince just looking at them. She glanced down the row of mirrors where she, Moira, Leila, Roisin and Mammy were lined up. 'We're like sitting ducks,' she'd heard Moira mumble as she flopped down into the chair and began to flick through a magazine for hairstyle ideas.

'I did, yes.' Aisling was prepared and she retrieved her bag from beside the chair where she'd put her carefully chosen cuttings from one of the bridal magazines, Leila had given her. The first picture she held up to show Tara was of a pretty blonde woman whose hair was slicked back and piled on her head in a loose top knot, flowers entwined in her hair, and Aisling thought the effect was ethereal.

'Nope.' Tara tapped her black booted toes on the floor. 'Won't work. Your face is too round.'

'I told her she'd look like Moonface with some sort of deposit on top of his head, you know yer funny little man from the *Faraway Tree* books, with that style,' Moira said to Tara.

Much to Aisling's satisfaction, Tara looked at Moira as though she'd flown in from Mars. She would have liked to kick her sister but she wasn't close enough and she wished she'd been quicker off the mark when they arrived at the salon; she'd have made sure Leila was sitting next to her.

'Let's see what else you've got there,' Tara said.

Aisling showed her the next one which was a half up, half down do of cascading waves.

'That's more like it.'

'Can I see.' Maureen poked her head forward trying to see past Roisin, Leila and Moira to where Aisling was sitting. She reminded Aisling of a turtle.

'Don't show her,' she hissed, but Maureen asked again only louder and Tara wasn't ready for a stand-off with the bolshie little woman down the end. Accordingly, the picture got passed down the line.

'No,' Maureen said shaking her head. 'Not with those ends of hers. Tara could you not give her a little snip.' She demonstrated with her thumb and index finger exactly how much she'd like her to take off Aisling's ends.

Tara looked at Aisling with an eyebrow raised questioningly and Aisling shook her head emphatically. 'Mammy,' she peered past her bridesmaids. 'I don't want my hair trimmed. I want it as long as possible on the day. I've been growing it, so I have.'

'But, Aisling, that's not a style.' She showed the picture to the stylist who'd drawn the short straw with Mammy on account of her being the youngest. 'Look, Polly, you can't call that a hairstyle, now can you?' Poor Polly looked like a rabbit caught in headlights. She was a girl who'd been raised not to argue with her mammy.

'Aisling, your woman there looks like she's been rolling around in the haystack prior to saying her nuptials with her intended.'

Aisling had had enough. 'Mammy, give that picture back right now. It's my wedding and my hair.'

Maureen reluctantly passed the picture to Roisin who handed it on. She turned to Polly and said, 'It's a sad day when your own daughter won't let you have a say in her wedding, so it is.'

Polly made a sympathetic sound and refused to look in Aisling's direction as she began to titivate Maureen's hair. Mercifully, Aisling saw she was distracted by Polly who was asking her what she had in mind.

'I was thinking curls, pin curls perhaps. I quite fancy the idea of looking like an olde worlde Hollywood starlet.'

'Bit long in the tooth for starlet, Mammy,' Moira said. 'Think *Golden Girls*, Polly.'

Roisin snorted. 'Curls? I told you, Mammy. It's a fact, people do begin to resemble their pets.'

'Not much hope for you then,' Moira bounced back with. 'Come to think of it, I can see the resemblance between you and Mr Nibbles. It's in the cheeks.'

It was the second time Moira missed receiving a kick on account of her sister not being able to reach.

Leila spoke up before the stylists could begin in earnest. 'We need to all have the same style obviously. Aisling what were you thinking?' She took charge.

'An updo of some description since I'm wearing mine half up and half down.'

'I'm mammy-of-the-bride,' Maureen piped up. 'I can have whatever style I want. Curls it is, Polly and don't you say another word on the subject.' She eyeballed Roisin.

Moira told Tegan, who was sensing her client might be trouble, that she didn't want anything severe. 'I was thinking more Andrea Corr so if we're to have it up think relaxed, bedhead that sort of thing,' she informed the stylist bossily.

'There'll be none of the bedhead, thank you very much, Tegan. I'll not have bedhead bridesmaids at a child of mine's wedding,' Maureen interrupted.

Tegan, Sten and Ciara, the stylists assigned to the bridesmaids, all froze and looked to Leila. She seemed the most sensible person here.

'Perhaps not bed hair but we don't have to go all out ballerina bun either.'

The three stylists all nodded and put their heads together murmuring in a hushed manner as they conferred. It was Sten who addressed them.

'I have suggested the latest updo that is storming Amsterdam.' His dark goatee quivered with excitement as he made his announcement. It looked at odds with the bleached crop of hair on his head and he was also clad head to toe in black.

Moira perked up. 'Amsterdam, well it's bound to be cool then. Go for it, Tegan.'

Leila agreed it sounded grand. Only Roisin was dubious but the Dutchman was somewhat intimidating so she wasn't about to argue. She watched as he began sorting through his trayful of hairstyling accessories with a studious expression on his face. She tried to relax in the seat but her shoulders, every-thing come to that, were tense and she realised her hands were in tight fists. The last time she'd let anyone near her hair it had been a disaster. Her fringe had wound up closer to her hairline than her eyebrows. It was not a look she wore well, although mercifully Shay hadn't seemed to notice. By the time it had finally grown back to a respectable length though she'd been sick to the back teeth of people talking to the expanse of forehead between her brows and fringe.

Think about Shay, she told herself and her fists unfurled; her shoulders too loosened at the memory of the night she'd spent with him. They'd met up once she'd gotten back from their successful outing to the Bridal Emporium. It had been so lovely to see him again and they'd gone for a quick bite to eat although neither of them could concentrate on the food placed in front of them as they stared into each other's eyes. A game of footsie under the table had ensued which had caused their breathing to quicken and pupils to dilate so they'd decided to skip dessert and had hotfooted it straight back to Shay's place for an entirely different and not so quick after dinner digestif.

Roisin's mouth curved into a smile she couldn't control as she recalled the way he'd propped himself up in bed on one el-bow afterward, looking down at her with a softness in his eyes that made her feel like she was the most beautiful creature to ever walk the earth. It was one of those moments she wished she could bottle so she could uncork it and relive the mem-ory on those lonely nights in London when Noah was at his father's and she found herself home alone. It was hard being in separate countries, even if they were only a hop, skip and a jump from each other. On the bright side of things though she'd be back in Dublin for the wedding in a fortnight. It wasn't too long to wait.

She realised Sten thought she was smiling at him and she noticed he'd sucked his stomach in because the slight paunch under his shirt had vanished. He was also pulling a moody pout in the mirror and looking at her in what he obviously thought was a flirtatious manner but which in Roisin's opinion gave him an unhinged look. Jaysus wept, just her luck she thought as her phone rang. The timing was perfect and she was grateful for the intrusion. She shot the Dutchman an apologetic glance. 'Sorry, Sten, I'll have to get this it could be my son or my boyfriend.' She wasn't missing the opportunity to say hello to either, even if it did make Sten's goatee quiver once more. He snorted huffily through his nostrils and began digging out bobby pins from his tray.

Roisin retrieved her phone from her bag and upon answering it was greeted by her son's sing-song voice. He was all excited to talk to her even though she'd only been away for a night and he spent every second weekend with his dad, anyway. It was lovely, Roisin thought feeling all warm inside and refusing to meet Sten's eyes in the mirror as he began tapping the comb he was holding in the palm of his hand as if to say, time is money. She listened to Noah fill her in on how much fun he was having. He'd been to see a film with his daddy and had been allowed an enormous bucket of popcorn. He didn't stop to draw breath as he informed her Granny Quealey was cooking him chicken nuggets with no vegetables not even a carrot for his dinner. Roisin rolled her eyes, that woman and her double standards.

'Where are you, Mummy?'

'I'm at the hairdressers with Aunty Aisling, Aunty Moira, your nana and Aisling's friend Leila. We're having a practise session to see how we're going to wear our hair on the day of the wedding.'

'Mummy?'

'Yes, Noah.'

'Can you please tell Nana she needs to look like Nana for the wedding.'

The poor child was still traumatised by his nana's post-Vietnam holiday braids, Roisin thought. 'I will.'

'Mummy, can you please do it now.'

'Alright, I'll hold the phone out so you can hear me tell her.' Roisin turned to Mammy whose hair was being clipped into a round coil. 'Noah's on the telephone, Mammy, and he says you're to look like you at Aisling's wedding.' She heard a tinny voice say, 'Tell Nana I used my manners, I said please.' 'He said please, Mammy.'

'Who else does he think I'm going to look like?' Maureen held out her hand. 'Here give that to me, I'll talk to him.'

Roisin passed it over and Sten took the opportunity to tug and twist Roisin's hair into the beginnings of a bun. He told her off for tilting her head, all business now he knew there was no chance of any post-hairdo shenanigans. She was straining to listen to what her mammy was saying to her son and managed to catch. 'Alright, Noah, Nana promises there'll be no teeny-tiny plaits and no Ronald McDonald fuzzy hair either. I can't wait to see you. Mammy's after telling me she's got your suit all sorted. Sure, you'll be the grandest pageboy who ever walked up the aisle, so you will. Oh, and before I go, be sure to tell Mr Nib-

bles, Nana loves him too. Yes, with all her heart. I'll pass you
back to your mammy now.'

Roisin took the phone back and said her goodbyes to her
son. She put her mobile back in her bag and decided she'd best
sit statue still from here on in. She wasn't risking annoying Sten
further. She'd learned the hard way, hairdressers wielded a lot
of power. Her eyes swivelled to her right but her head didn't
move as she looked at Mammy in the mirror. To use Aisling's
favourite turn of phrase, she was such a fecky brown noser. All
that business about being sure to tell Mr Nibbles I love him.
She was only saying it to get one up on Noah's Granny Quealey.
If the gerbil found his way into her undergarments, he'd be history. She returned her gaze to the mirror in front of her to see
what was happening to her hair. Oh, dear God, what was Sten
doing? She was beginning to resemble a praying mantis. What
were those pieces of hair he'd pulled loose doing? They looked
like tentacles for feck's sake.

'You like it?' he asked, catching her eye in the mirror. 'Like
I said, this look is hot, hot, hot in Holland.'

Well it could fecking well stay in Holland, Roisin thought,
looking to her sister and Leila who were looking back at her,
eyes wide with alarm.

Um, perhaps we could have something a little more traditional?' Aisling asked upon seeing her bridesmaids. 'Something
a little more...' she tried to find the word she was looking for
but Moira jumped in for her.

'Something more human and less insect-like would be
good.'

Chapter 14

Maureen was the first out of the doors of Hair She Goes and she announced to Aisling, Roisin, Moira and Leila who followed that she would head home from there. 'I've a dog who'll be desperate to see me and he'll need a walk before we paint the town red.'

'But your curls will drop in the damp sea air, Mammy,' Aisling pointed out.

'I thought of that, Aisling, I'll wear a headscarf.'

'And will you show everyone you pass on your walk your wartime ration card, Mammy.' Moira said.

'Don't be clever with me, young lady. And if you'd paid attention in your history classes at school, you'd know Ireland was neutral in the war. Besides, it wasn't me who was after looking like she belonged on a twig in the Amazonian rain forest.'

Moira couldn't think of a comeback because Mammy was right. At least middle ground had been reached and the antennae were no more. They were all relatively happy with the outcome, especially Aisling, which was the main thing, Leila had pointed out once the stylists had stepped back to admire their handiwork.

Roisin rubbed her scalp, Sten had been unnecessarily firm with the pulling of her hair and placement of bobby pins once he'd learned she had a boyfriend and there would be no riding happening once the salon closed. She, for one, was glad to be out of there.

Arrangements were made for Mammy and Leila to be back at O'Mara's later that evening for drinks, hen party games and, what Moira promised would be plenty of craic, before the limousine came to pick them up and take them out on the town. With that, the bride and her two sisters made their way back to the guesthouse.

The trio piled in through the door, giggling, a short while later. 'What's so funny?' James asked looking wary. The student manned the front desk on a weekend during the day while Evie, a fellow student, did the evening shift. She'd be on board in forty minutes at four pm. He wished it was four o'clock now. Giggling groups of women like this made him nervous.

'What do you think of our hair, James?' Moira asked, patting hers.

'You all look the same.' He'd yet to grasp that women preferred more flowery nuances.

'That's the idea,' Roisin said. 'We've been for a trial run at the hairdressers for Aisling's wedding.'

'Oh right.' James looked down at the fax he'd taken off the machine, studying it as though it might explain the workings of the female mind. He got the feeling a compliment of some sort was in order so he dug deep and came up with. 'Well, you all look grand.'

'Thank you, James,' Moira said, sensing it was as good as they were going to get. She led the way toward the stairs but before she got there, she spied the guests from room eight sitting in the guest lounge. Mr and Mrs Dunbar had arrived for a long weekend in the fair city yesterday morning for no reason other than they'd always fancied exploring Dublin. They were a chatty couple with broad Scottish accents who said things like dinnae and laddie and lassie a lot. They hailed from a village near Edinburgh and Moira had whiled away a good half hour talking with them while she herded Aisling and Bronagh up and down the stairs yesterday morning. They'd said their goodbyes when Bronagh, red in the face, had threatened Moira with bodily harm if she made her do it again. 'Hello again, Mr and Mrs Dunbar.' She paused to smile at the older couple although Mr Dunbar was oblivious given he'd nodded off in the wingback chair. The hairs of his bushy moustache were blowing with each little snore she noticed as Mrs Dunbar waved over, a cup of tea in her hand.

'Hullo, Moira. We're not long back from doing the hop-on hop-off bus tour and now we're enjoying a well-earned cup of tea, or at least I am. We've been on the go all day and we're dead on our feet.' She gestured toward her husband. 'As you can see.' The sweet-faced woman with faded red hair that curled at her chin smiled at the small group gathered in the doorway. 'Did I overhear you lassies telling the wee laddie on the front desk you'd been having your hair done as a trial run for a wedding?'

'Yes, it's my wedding, Mrs Dunbar,' Aisling said, pushing past Moira into the lounge. She wanted to go and see Quinn but she always had time to chat with their guests.

'Call me Maggie, dearie.'

Aisling smiled.

'Well, don't you look a bonnie lassie with those flowers in your hair. Now, what is it my grandson says when something's good?' She looked to her husband who gave a rumbling snore followed by a whistling sound. 'Fat lot of good you are. It'll come to me.' She screwed her bright blue eyes up trying to find the words and then her face brightened. 'Pure barry, that's it.

Your hair looks pure barry, Aisling. Mine used to be that colour when I was younger believe it or not. And you two bonnie lassies are the bridesmaids I take it?'

Roisin and Moira nodded.

'Come in and have a blether about these wedding plans of yours,' she invited.

They weren't in any rush and so Roisin played mother making the tea while Aisling sat down on the sofa with Moira chatting away to the friendly Scots woman. She told her all about the latest look in Holland that had her bridesmaids resembling praying mantises. Mrs Dunbar was chuckling away at the picture Aisling was painting when Roisin, dunking a teabag into a cup, interrupted and told them all about Sten misinterpreting her expression and how he'd not had the lightest of touches after she'd made it clear she was spoken for. They all laughed as she relayed how his goatee quivered when he got excited or annoyed.

'Oh, and what about Mammy,' Moira snorted, mimicking her informing her poor stylist, Polly that she was the mammy of the bride and as such could wear her hair, however which way she wanted.

'Mother of the bride is a lovely thing to be indeed. My hair was on my shoulders when my daughter got married, I had it blow waved and set for her big day and wore a magenta hat with my dress. Navy it was with a magenta rose pattern. What did your mammy decide to do with her hair?'

'Curls, Maggie.' Aisling said. 'And for some reason when I think of Mammy's curls I want to start singing and doing a spot of the tap-dancing,' Aisling said.

All eyes turned toward her, unsure what she was on about.

She got up from the sofa beginning to jig about as she burst into song. *On the Good Ship Lollipop*, she tapped away.

'Shirley Temple!' Maggie clapped delightedly. 'She went for ringlets then.'

'They were supposed to be pin curls but they were very tight. The drizzle out there should sort them out though, even if she does wear a headscarf over them.' Aisling gestured to the large windows facing the street from where they could see a glimpse of the glistening, slick pavement outside before sitting back down again.

Roisin carried two cups of tea over and as she started laughing, they rattled ominously on the saucers.

'What's so funny?' Moira asked.

She managed to set the tea down in front of her sisters without spilling it and took centre stage in the room before launching into her heartfelt take on *Tomorrow*.

'Little Orphan Annie!' Mrs Dunbar chortled, thoroughly enjoying this impromptu version of charades.

The giggles were getting loud and James poked his head around the door to see what was going on. He shook his head on seeing a room full of women and a snoring man. It reminded him of when his mammy got together with her sisters, and his da always nodded off thanks to the extra glass of whisky he'd have knocked back in order to cope with his sisters-in-law.

Moira wasn't going to be left out. 'My turn.' She stood up and began to perform some fancy footwork while singing Michael Jackson's *ABC*. The others were in fits and when poor Mr Dunbar woke himself up with a particularly violent snore he had to blink rapidly because he'd found himself in a room full of giggling women. And what he'd like to know was why was the bonnie lassie he'd been speaking to yesterday dancing around singing a song he hadn't heard since the seventies? They were a mad lot these Irish, he thought, reaching for his cup of tea.

Chapter 15

Aisling swept into the house in Blanchardstown that Quinn shared with his mam and dad, glad to be in out of the cold. She'd felt like your character from the Narnia book the half human, half horse one that got frozen as she waited for the bus. Now, the homely smell of fabric softener and fresh baking washed over her. She greeted her soon-to-be mammy-in-law with a big fecky brown noser smile and received a warm one in return. She'd known Mrs Moran since her student days and was very fond of her but lately she'd found herself feeling irritated by her fiancé's mam's incessant fussing over Quinn. He wasn't a baby, he was a grown man and it was ridiculous the way she ran after him.

Quinn's siblings had all long since left home, as had he until he decided to open his bistro. It was a decision that saw him leave behind his career in London to move back to Dublin. He hadn't intended to move home but given the soaring accommodation costs in the city and the uncertainty of trying to get a new business off the ground, it had been the sensible thing to do. Sometimes, Aisling thought he'd gotten a little too used to being back in the family fold. She expected them to be a partnership when they finally moved in together at O'Mara's, the sensible option given Aisling needed to be on site and Quinn's bistro was a hop, skip and a jump away, and began their married life. You would not find her waiting on her new husband hand and foot the way Mrs Moran was prone to doing with her husband and sons.

Of course, it wasn't all down to her. Quinn seemed perfectly happy to let his mammy do so. She'd broached the subject with him a few weeks back but he'd shrugged in that laid-back way of his that was at times endearing and at times frustrating and said, 'I think she feels she has to prove herself after her stroke, you know. She likes to feel needed.'

Aisling had blustered back, 'But that's silly.'

'Aisling,' Quinn had said in a way that suggested she was very naïve when it came to the stuff of life. 'Sometimes it's easier to go with the flow than to upset someone over things that don't matter in the big picture.' She'd had the feeling he was talking about her and hadn't pressed it further, not wanting to hear something she might not like.

'How're you, Mrs Moran,' Aisling asked now, noting she had her customary shamrock apron tied around her waist.

'Aisling dear, I've told you a million times you're family. It's Maeve and I'm very well although I'm having problems getting the stains out of Quinn's chef whites. I'm after trying vinegar and baking soda.'

Aisling wished her mammy could hear this conversation. Not the part about slaving over Quinn's whites, the other part, because it was her fault she struggled with being on a first name basis with her soon to be in-laws. It had indeed been ingrained in her to address her elders with a Mr, Mrs or Aunty this or that. Perhaps she should go for the middle ground and call Mrs Moran, Mrs Maeve. 'Have you been baking? It smells wonderful in here.' She was only being polite because Mrs Maeve was always after whipping something up in that kitchen of hers. This house was a dieting woman's worst nightmare.

'I have and you're in luck. There's a batch of biscuit brownies fresh out of the oven, that's if Quinn's not eaten them all.'

Aisling groaned inwardly. Mrs Maeve's biscuit brownies were the best.

'They're his favourites as you know,' the little woman continued. She reached out and rested a hand on Aisling's forearm to waylay her a moment longer. Her voice dropped almost conspiratorially. 'When you've a moment, Aisling I'll show you how to bake them, I've been making notes of all his favourite foods for you because you know how the saying goes. The way to a man's heart—'

'Is through his stomach,' Aisling finished for her. Mr Moran had told her the other day he was on the fence about his son finally leaving home because he was sure the baked goods on offer would go downhill.

'You'll find Quinn in the kitchen going over his books. Oh, I nearly forgot. How did you get on with your hair appointment?' She looked at Aisling's hair which was flowing loose as per her usual style. She'd taken all the bobby pins and woven flowers out once back at the guesthouse. She didn't want to ruin the surprise on her wedding day. She patted her hair self-consciously and told Mrs Maeve this.

'And your dress, did you find what you wanted?'

The thought of her beautiful dress made Aisling smile. 'I did and I love it, it's perfect.' She quickly added. 'You know you were welcome to come along with us. My mammy was saying she'd like to get to know you better, now we're all going to be family. Are you sure I can't tempt you to join us tonight too?'

'I must organise a lunch for us all and it was thoughtful of you to include me, Aisling, but sure you know how tired I can get when I'm out and about too long and you didn't need me huffing and puffing about the place. As for a hen night, I've not got the stamina.' Maeve felt guilty seeing the earnest expression on Aisling's face. She was telling the truth about not having the stamina for this evening's festivities but the truth of why she hadn't gone along to help Aisling choose her dress was because her future daughter-in-law was so frazzled of late. She'd only met Maureen a handful of times too and she'd been worried about treading on toes, or saying the wrong thing to Aisling. Not that she'd told Quinn that of course.

'I wouldn't have minded.' She didn't want her future mammy-in-law to feel pushed out of things because this wedding was as much about her son as it was about Aisling and her side of the family.

'Well I'm sure you're going to be the most beautiful bride, Dublin's ever seen, dear. And sure, you'll have a grand time tonight. It will do you good to let your hair down. You'll find Cathal on his chair in the front room if you want to pop your head in and say hello. I'd best get back to the whites.'

Mrs Maeve scuttled off and Aisling ventured into the front room where Mr Moran was reclining in his La-Z-Boy chair with a newspaper held open in front of him.

'Hello there,' she called, stooping down to pet Tabatha the cat who'd gotten up from her corner of the sofa in order to greet her. The cat rubbed against her legs purring loudly as Mr Moran lowered his paper and peered over top of it. 'Hello there, yourself, Aisling. How're you doing?'

'Grand thanks, yourself?'

'Oh, I can't complain.'

Aisling noticed the cup of tea with a piece of the brownie tucked in alongside it on the saucer on the side table next to where he was sitting, and picturing his wife buzzing around making sure he was comfortable thought, no you can't. It's the life of Riley you're after living. He was a lovely man but he was also a solid, lazy, lump of a man and woe betide Quinn if he made noises about purchasing a La-Z-Boy chair when he moved into O'Mara's.

'All set for tonight, then?' she asked, referencing Quinn's stag do. Hugh, the oldest of the Moran boys, was to be his baby brother's best man and it was in this role that he'd organised the stag do. Aisling was pleased about this because Hugh at forty, married with four sons of his own, was a sensible family man unlike the two middle Morans, Ivo and Rowan, neither of whom was married and both of whom who had long-suffering girlfriends. Aisling would never say it to Quinn but she'd mentally given the two eejity brothers the nicknames of Lloyd and Harry from the Jim Carey film, *Dumb and Dumber*.

'I'm conserving my energy, Aisling, in order to keep up with the young ones.'

'Fair play to you, Mr Moran.'

'Call me Cathal, for goodness sake, Aisling.'

'Sorry.'

'You're too polite for your own good, so you are.' He grinned to soften his words before vanishing behind his paper once more. She took her cue to leave him to it and with a final tickle behind Tabitha's ear ventured off to the kitchen to find Quinn.

He was sitting at the big family-sized pine table about to stuff a piece of the biscuit brownie in his gob. Spread out in front of him were the books from the bistro and he looked up with a sheepish grin when he saw Aisling in the doorway.

'Caught me.'

'I'm betting it's not your first piece either.' Her eyes flitted to where the tray was on top of the oven. The slab of the chocolate treat was missing quite a few pieces.

'No comment. Can I tempt you?' He gestured toward the oven and she frowned as her mouth watered at the thought of it. Quinn did not make her efforts to lose a few pounds before the fourteenth of February, easy.

She focussed on her dress and the need to be able to slide that zipper up and down with ease. 'No, thanks. I won't.

Quinn shovelled the brownie down as though frightened it might be taken off him. He wouldn't it put it past her, she'd been kind of crazy lately in the build-up to this bloody wedding of theirs. He'd seen her checking out his middle the other day and did not want to find himself being ordered to do a crash course of the Weight Watchers. He pushed his chair back and patted his knee. She went and sat down slipping her arms around his neck.

'I wanted to see you before tonight.'

'Why do you look so worried?'

'I don't, do I?'

'Yeah, you do and you know you don't need to be. We're going for a meal and a few drinks that's it. There won't be any strippers or that sort of carry on, you know that, not with Hugh having organised it. Ivo and Rowan were all for it but I put my foot down. It's my stag night and that isn't my bag.

Besides, Dad would be mortified if anyone waggled any naked bits under his nose.'

The two middle brothers went up a notch in the eejit stakes. They were elevated from mere eejits to super eejits. Hugh however was allocated a halo.

'I'm not worried, I trust you. I feel edgy, I suppose.' Aisling paused, unsure how far she should go. Quinn had told her often enough that she had nothing to worry about where he was concerned, he loved her. She knew all this in the logical part of her brain but still there was this feeling she couldn't shake that somehow things would go wrong. She decided not to put her fears into words. She didn't want to put a dampener on his evening. She wanted him to enjoy himself tonight and not be worrying about his overly sensitive wife-to-be.

'Do you know what I think your problem is,' he said, nuzzling her neck.

'Don't do that, your mammy might walk in.'

He paused in his nuzzling. 'You're hungry, Ash. Have a piece of that brownie, it'll sort you out so it will.' He was teasing her.

'Ah, ignore me and my moaning, I'm grand and I do not, read my lips, do not need the brownie.'

He looked sceptical but didn't push matters. 'And what about you, what's Leila got planned for you? Is it the Chippendales you'll be going to see or have those Riverdance fellows ventured into the murky waters of Irish dancing with nothing but a bow tie on to keep them warm?'

Aisling screwed her face up. 'God Almighty, Quinn. That would give me nightmares so it would. All those high kicks, it doesn't bear thinking about.'

He laughed.

'So far as I know, Leila's organised a few drinks at O'Mara's with party games then we've a limousine picking us up to take us for a meal and onto a few pubs.'

'Does the unsuspecting Dublin public know your mammy and Bronagh are being let loose on the town?'

Aisling elbowed him playfully, her mood lifting. It was one of the things she loved most about him, his ability to make her laugh. She kissed him full on the lips, suddenly uncaring if his mammy were to walk in on them. 'I love you very much, Quinn Moran.'

'And I love you, Aisling O'Mara.'

Chapter 16

Maureen could hear the phone ringing as she turned the key in her lock and she pushed the door open before stampeding over to answer it. She could murder a cup of tea but it would have to wait, she thought as Pooh managed to get caught up around her legs in his haste to get to the laundry. He was desperate to see what was on offer in his food bowl. Cursing, she let go of his leash and righted herself before she hit the deck. Thoroughly flustered, she grasped hold of the receiver and answered it with a breathy, 'Hello.'

'Hello there, yourself, Maureen. How're you doing on this wet and wild afternoon?'

She smiled upon hearing the voice at the other end and forgot all about her coveted cup of tea and the high drama she'd had trying to get to the phone. She relieved herself of her rain jacket carrying it through to the laundry to hang up. 'I'm very well, Donal. Thank you for asking.' She was frozen to the bone after braving the elements on Howth Harbour but his cheery voice warmed her as much as the central heating would do. He brought out her generous side which was lucky for Pooh because she held the phone to her ear while scooping a load of dried biscuits into his bowl with her free hand. It wasn't his dinnertime for another hour, and the poodle's tail wagged at this unexpected bonus. Leaving him to enjoy his food, Maureen took herself back to the warmth of the living room and, kicking off her shoes, she settled herself down for a cosy chat.

Donal was a glass half-full man with an unfailingly positive attitude and he was exactly the sort of person she wanted to spend time with these days. Life was too short to find yourself on the arm of a crotchety old man and, thought Maureen, it was astounding the number of querulous men in their late sixties roaming the streets of Dublin at any given time. It was not something she'd noticed when her Brian was alive but once she'd been widowed a respectable length of time, they seemed to have come crawling out of the woodwork moaning and groaning all the way.

Sure, there'd they be with their walking slacks pulled up high around their armpits, their waistlines a thing of the past, as they complained at the rambling group get togethers how the price of gas was going up yet again and how was a pensioner supposed to keep warm in this godforsaken country of theirs? Or, at her painting class they'd be moaning the paperboy had tossed the newspaper onto the damp grass again and how was a man supposed to find out what was happening in the world when the front page was soggy? Oh, and she'd never come up for air again if she were to start on the curmudgeonly lot down at the bowls who were always on about how hard it was to get a decent cup of tea these days as they sipped their brew at the afternoon break.

Donal brought her back to the here and now. 'I'm ringing for no other reason than I wanted to hear your voice.'

It was rather nice to have someone want to hear the sound of her voice for a change.

'Have you had a good day?' he asked.

'I have.' She remembered her curls and would have liked him to see them. She raised a hand to fluff her hair up and realised she still had the headscarf on. 'I've not long walked in the door. I was after taking Pooh for a walk down the pier. It was very invigorating, so it was.'

'I'd say it would be. I very much enjoyed our walk the other day.'

'I did too, and I'm sorry about Pooh. He's not used to male company and he can be quite territorial where I'm concerned.' She'd been mortified when the poodle had cocked his leg and before she'd been able to stop him, peed on Donal's left trainer.

Donal laughed his big rumbly laugh. 'There's a first time for everything, Maureen, and sure he'll get used to me.'

She liked the way Donal was planning on being around enough for Pooh to get to know him. But as quickly as the warm fuzzy feeling had come it went and she felt queasy as though she'd been eating too much rich, fried food. If he was planning on winning her poodle over, it wouldn't be long before he was making noises about meeting her girls and introducing her to his girls. She wasn't sure if she was ready for that yet. It would make things official. It would open him up to judgment from her three because it would be inevitable, they'd draw comparisons between him and their father. Just as it was inevitable Donal's two daughters would compare her to their late mammy. Neither of them were looking for a replacement for their late spouses though. Through no choice of their own they'd found themselves on their own. It was a lonely thing to turn to tell someone something and find there was no one there anymore. This wasn't something she thought either of their children would understand.

Her girls, she knew, had been gobsmacked by her New Year's Eve announcement of having made a new man friend.

They were itching to know more about him too but so far, every time she'd sensed they were about to pump her for information, she'd managed to head them off. She wouldn't get away with it much longer and she supposed she didn't want to either because she liked Donal. She liked him a lot; she only hoped they would too and she didn't even want to think about what Donal's girls would make of her.

She could feel Brian's eyes on her from where he gazed out of the silver frame watching over her living room. She liked to think he'd approve, not that there was anything to disapprove of. Thus far, she and Donal had met for lunch and gone for walks and spoken on the phone but there'd been no romantic encounters. She wasn't sure how she'd fare were he to make such an advance but she certainly wouldn't be averse, to him trying. Was kissing and the rest of it like riding a bike? Did it all come back to you once you got back in the saddle so to speak?

'I'm sure he will, Donal,' she said, spying Pooh licking his chops, his dinner finished as he moseyed toward her. 'What do you think about coming along with me to the puppy training class next week? It might help.'

'I'd be honoured to accompany you.'

Again, Maureen smiled, hugging the sound of his jovial voice to her before inquiring as to what he'd spent the day doing.

'I had a grand morning looking after my Gaby's little Keegan.' They whiled away a half hour chatting about the delights of being a grandparent and then, glancing at her watch, Maureen realised she needed to think about getting ready. She had a big evening ahead of her.

'I'll ring you tomorrow then, Maureen. I'm looking forward to hearing all the craic of the hen night,' Donal said.

'It will be down to me and Bronagh to keep an eye on proceedings. We'll make sure things don't get out of control,' she informed him before ringing off and floating her way over to the kitchen. She flicked the kettle on and popped a teabag in a cup before sitting down at the table to wait for the kettle to boil. Her mind flitted back to Donal and she played over, as she'd done so at least one hundred times or more, the yacht club Christmas dinner where she'd first met him.

She'd set such high store on the evening but the night was promising to be a flop and she was regretting all the effort she'd gone to having her hair and nails done. Rosemary Farrell had agreed to be her plus one for the evening, even though she didn't belong to the club, and Maureen was grateful to her for agreeing to accompany her. She'd learned since Brian had passed a lot of married women didn't take kindly to a widow joining them at their table. She imagined it would be the same for the newly divorced. Rosemary however had managed to wear her gratitude at keeping her company thin by the time they'd finished their, pre-dinner drinks with her complaining about her clicking hip.

Maureen had sat down at their allocated table for the meal and two men she'd met a handful of times while taking her sailing lessons had swooped down to sit either side of her. Rosemary and her clicking hip never stood a chance. Instead, her rambling club friend sat down across the table next to a woman who worked for the council. Rosemary, Maureen had seen glancing over, was in her apple cart at having an ear to bend about the state of some of the public walking ways. She'd gotten particularly strident as she informed the council woman how she was sure the shoddy paths had played a part in giving her a dicky hip in the first place. Maureen felt sorry for the woman, knowing she was in for a blow by blow account of Rosemary's hip replacement surgery over their entrees.

So it was, Maureen found herself sandwiched between Grady Macaleese, an aging playboy who had a penthouse overlooking the harbour here in Howth. He'd droned on and on about his boating prowess in a manner which had made her wonder whether he was talking about boating at all. He'd kept mentioning things like his big rudder and his ramrod boom. On her right was Rory Power, a wet-lipped, ruddy-cheeked man with an appalling combover who'd not been able to avert his eyes from her bosom all evening. It was a miracle how his fork had managed to find his mouth during the main course.

Yes, she'd been wondering why she'd bothered coming and she'd been so looking forward to the evening too. She liked mingling with the boatie types, just not these two boatie eejits. As the plates were cleared away and Grady began to tell her about how he liked to manhandle his keel, she looked toward the stage and her mood brightened. The band was about to start. At least she wouldn't be able to hear him over the music. She interrupted him, past caring if he thought her rude. 'What sort of music are we in for?'

Grady looked flummoxed at having to answer a question not directly related to himself. Rory, eyes still firmly attached to Maureen's right breast, informed her it was to be a Kenny Rogers tribute band. 'The club's director of entertainment is a country and western fan, that's him prancing around in the cowboy boots, over there.' He pointed toward the stage.

Oh yes, Maureen thought, spying the gentleman in question, all he was missing was a piece of straw to chew on. She liked the sound of some Kenny Rogers though. *The Gambler* usually got everyone on their feet.

It had too, she thought now, getting to her feet as she heard the kettle begin bubbling away. She'd managed to escape the clutches of Grady and Rory by taking herself off to the bathroom and when she'd reappeared, she'd attached herself to a large group who'd taken to the dance floor. She'd felt a little like a teenager as she caught the eye of the singer who did indeed have a look of your man Kenny with his thick thatch of salt and pepper hair and matching beard. It was his twinkling eyes that won her over though and when he asked if he could fetch her a drink while the band took their break, she was very happy to accept. Rosemary's nose had been out of joint when she'd spotted Maureen in conversation with the lead singer whose name, she'd since found out, was Donal. She'd limped over to say she was calling it a night because there was no show of her being able to manage the dancing, not with her hip clicking.

Maureen poured the boiled water into her cup and waited for the tea to brew. She wondered what her children would make of Donal's retirement hobby. Sure, she decided, they'd be won over like she'd been if they got the chance to hear him sing *Lucille*. Satisfied her tea was just the right shade of tannin, she flicked the bag onto the little saucer she kept beside the kettle and then carried her drink over to the table. Pooh began to whine as she burst into the Dolly part of *Islands in the Stream*. It was something she'd been doing ever since she'd met Donal.

Chapter 17

'Moira O'Mara, I can see your knickers!' Maureen said. She was perched on the edge of the sofa in the living room of the family apartment in between Bronagh and Ita. They were all awaiting the appearance of the bride-to-be. She'd opted for a slimline tonic, mixed with the gin her eyes had migrated to when she'd arrived, and it was going down a treat. Bronagh, who'd poured herself into a deep pink dress, which she told Maureen she'd had a sod of job trying to match a lipstick with, informed her she'd brought the gin along. The hidden calories in those pre-mix lolly water drinks all the young ones were so keen on knocking back would make your hair curl, she'd said, thinking herself hilarious given Maureen's curls. She was still chortling to herself as she reached forward to help herself to the cheese and crackers. It was the second time Maureen had had to slap Bronagh's hand away, telling her she'd regret her poor snack choices in the morning.

Nina had also joined them for the evening and was looking forward to a rare night out. It wasn't often she got to be a young woman with no responsibilities or cares and she intended to have fun. Mrs Flaherty had declined Aisling's invitation on the grounds of her bedtime being nine pm these days and young Evie who worked the weekend evening shift on reception, was precisely that, young.

'You can't,' Moira said, craning her neck to look back over her shoulder. She'd been standing by the dining table chatting to Aisling's old work friends when Maureen had caught sight of her skirt and nearly spilled her G&T.

'I can. They're purple and barely cover that arse of yours.'

'Well it is a hen night, Mammy. We're supposed to cause all sorts of trouble around the town. And what do you call the get-up you've on?'

'The only trouble you'll be getting, my girl, is the back of my hand on your bare legs. Now go and put something suitable on. I'll not have a daughter of mine flashing her knickers to all and sundry.' Maureen flicked her hand in the direction of the hallway, shooing her off.

Moira ignored her, knowing it would take too much energy for Mammy to get up from the sofa to smack the back of her legs. Her glory days of being fast as lightning with the wooden spoon were over. She took in her mammy's white cowboy boots and her eyes travelled upward. 'Jaysus, Mammy, please tell me those aren't rhinestones on your blouse.' She was wearing a black skirt, nothing wrong with that. It was a perfectly respectable knee length teamed with a long-sleeved silky black blouse which revealed a tad too much cleavage in Moira's opinion. One Cindy in the family was enough. It was the sparkly, swirly pattern across the chest she took umbrage with. It looked very much like rhinestones. All she needed was a big fecky off, cowboy hat, big blonde hair, enormous boobs, a smaller waist and the ability to hold a note, and she'd be like an Irish Dolly Parton.

'They're diamantes not rhinestones.'

'You're like a grandmotherly version of Madonna changing your look every fecking few minutes,' Moira muttered.

Maureen lunged forward and Moira scooted around the other side of the table, smirking as she saw Mammy was all hot air. She hadn't managed to make it out of the seat.

'Enough of the language on your sister's special night,' she said, settling back on the cushions and giving her gin and tonic, the attention it was due.

Ita looked down at her carefully chosen black dress with its white polka dots, bought specially for this evening from River Island. It had cost her nearly a week's wages and she'd teemed it with black knee-high boots as the shop assistant had suggested. She'd felt a million dollars when she'd left home earlier, her mam's voice ringing in her ears. 'Be sure to remember me to Maureen, now Ita.' She'd wanted to impress the O'Mara sisters who only ever saw her pushing a cleaning trolley about the place. She felt certain they looked down their haughty noses at her and she'd planned on showing them she scrubbed up as well as the next girl. Now though, looking at Moira in her tiny scarlet skirt she felt frumpy, as though she were off to a church social and not on a hen night. Her stomach knotted in the way it always did when she was around the O'Mara sisters.

Bronagh put in her penny's worth. 'Moira, if you prance around the city streets in that skirt, you'll be offered money in return for favours. Mark my words.'

Moira frowned, not sure what Bronagh was on about, her mammy's message had come across loud and clear though. 'What I want to know, Mammy, is why it's alright for you to swan around the city in your yoga pants showing everyone your bits but I can't wear a short skirt when I'm in the prime of my youth.'

'The yoga pants are very good for the mobility so they are. I can bend and stretch and get in and out of the car and remember, young lady, you'll still be my daughter when you're sixty and past your so-called prime. Besides, I'm after getting a new pair. It won't be me flashing my undergarments to anyone who cares to take a look.'

Roisin looked up from where she was scooping paté onto a cracker over by the kitchen worktop. 'What do you mean you've got a new pair?' Her eyes narrowed. 'Mammy, have you been nosing in my suitcase?'

Nina was sitting in the armchair near the windows and her head swivelled back and forth, like a tennis ball being thwacked across the court, between the sisters and their mother. She would never answer back to her madre the way these girls did theirs but she envied their easy relationship with her too.

Maureen had a shifty expression on her face but before Roisin could grill her further, Leila appeared looking glamorous in a silver halter neck dress.

'Leila, you look a picture, so you do,' Maureen exclaimed, grateful for the diversion.

'Thank you, Maureen, but wait until you see our bride. Aisling,' she called.

Aisling came striding out with her hands on her hips as though strutting the catwalk. Roisin whistled and Maureen and Bronagh clapped. Aisling's two girlfriends from her resort management days, Rowena call me Ro-ro and Tina-Marie like Lisa-Marie Presley only it's Tina-Marie Preston, cheered. Aisling was stunning in a sage green chiffon strappy number with impossibly high Louboutins and a fluffy white veil pinned into her hair. A drink was pressed into her hand and she took a seat alongside her old friends as Moira took charge.

'Has everyone got a drink?'

'Yes,' came the chorused reply.

'Good, because we've a few presents there on the table for Aisling to open and then I thought we could play some games before our limousine whisks us away. I thought we'd start with Bridal Bingo.'

'I love that,' Ro-ro squealed turning to Tina-Marie. 'It's great craic. I played it last month at Stephanie's hen night. Aisling you should sit at the head of the table to open your presents.'

Aisling pulled out the chair and dutifully sat down.

'Go and change that skirt, Moira,' Maureen bossed.

Seeing she was going to get no peace until she did, she told the expectant hens she'd be two ticks before racing off to the bedroom. She reappeared with a skirt that came down to the middle of her shapely thighs. 'Better, Mammy?'

'Much better.' Maureen was appeased. She was also enjoying her gin and tonic. It had been years since she'd tippled on that particular mixer. 'Bronagh, how's your drink there. Shall I top us up?'

'A grand idea, Maureen.' Bronagh said. 'Help me up would you, Ita?'

Ita took her hand and heaved the receptionist up from the sofa. They all gathered around the table, Maureen watching the proceedings from where she was sloshing tonic into a generous measure of gin.

'Open this one first, Aisling,' Roisin said, sliding a large shiny wrapped package toward her sister. 'It's from me and Moira.'

Aisling tore the paper off and stared at the wedding advent calendar inside. Little bags of varying sizes in different girly pink fabrics were pinned to the board in a two-week count-down between now and her big day. 'Did you two make this?'

The sisters nodded beaming. 'All the little bags were sewn by hand,' Roisin affirmed.

Aisling blinked back tears not wanting her mascara to run. 'It's fantastic, thank you. When did you get the time?'

'We've been making the bags for weeks and sorting the lit-tle gifts inside, but we put it all together when you shot off to see Quinn after we'd been to the Bridal Emporium yesterday.'

'Well, I love it.'

'Open number fourteen,' Moira bossed, and Aisling delved into the pink gingham bag accordingly. Inside was a voucher. 'It's for a pedicure, ah thanks, Moira, Rosi.' She got up and hugged her sisters. 'That's not all we got you, open this one.' Moira picked up a small, soft package and passed it to Aisling.

She ripped off the paper, in the swing of things now, and found two pairs of knickers, one in red lace the other black. 'Jaysus wept,' she said holding them up. 'They're tiny so they are.'

'And what do you call those? There's no gusset in them. Sure, what's the point?' Bronagh said taking the gin and tonic Maureen handed to her and slurping on it.

'Crotchless panties, Bronagh. Which is exactly the point.'

Bronagh spluttered on her gin, making the others laugh.

'And I made you this.' Maureen gave her the scrapbook chronicling her daughter's life to date. She'd spent many a happy evening tripping down memory lane putting it together for Aisling, having done the same for Roisin when she got married.

'I'll treasure it, Mammy, thank you.'

Leila began to leaf through it exclaiming over Aisling in her first communion dress. 'Sure, your dress reminds me of Princess Diana's wedding dress.'

Aisling ploughed through the rest of the gifts which ranged from a bottle of Tahitian massage oil to a box of pink champagne truffles which she duly passed around.

Moira cleared the wrapping paper from the table and said, 'Aisling, can you fill this sheet out with words related to your wedding. Everybody else, did you fill in the cards I gave you earlier?'

There was a collective 'yes' and Aisling got busy writing. 'Finished,' she said, and Moira checked the group was ready with their pens before telling her to start calling out what she'd written.

'Cake,' she said, hearing the frantic clicking of ballpoint pens before carrying on with the rest of her random wedding words. It was when she called, 'Garter belt,' that Ita jumped up and shouted, 'Bingo!'

Moira handed her a decorative bottle stopper as her prize.

Maureen and Bronagh's competitive streaks put in an appearance during the ensuing game of Prosecco Pong with Maureen demonstrating an uncanny talent for getting the ping pong ball in the cup.

'We've time for one last game,' Moira said checking her watch. 'What shall it be, ladies? The Cocktail Quiz or True or False.'

The Cocktail Quiz won.

It turned out Nina had an extensive knowledge of cocktails, thanks to her background in hospitality. She was gifted a canvas pouch which Leila told her was for keeping life's little necessities in.

'I haven't had a cocktail in a good while. The pina colada was always my go-to. I wouldn't mind one tonight.'

'Mammy, you haven't lived until you've tried a Cosmopolitan,' Moira said, glancing at her watch and announcing the limousine would be pulling up downstairs in approximately five minutes.

There was a flurry of last-minute organisation on the part of the bride-to-be and her flushed-cheeked guests in the form of lip gloss application, calls of nature, and the checking of bags for keys. Sorted, they made their way toward the door only to find Moira blocking the exit as she held up a large shopping bag. 'Before we go,' she said, 'I need you all to wear these.'

There was laughter, especially when Maureen announced if it was anything rude like willies bobbing about on a headband, you could count her out.

'Me too, I'm not wearing the pink, glittery willies on my head at my age,' Bronagh said, backing her up.

'It's traditional for the hen party to wear sashes or badges, or even crowns, not willies on headbands, Mammy and Bronagh. However, Leila, Rosi and I have gone one better. Close your eyes everybody,' Moira ordered, and they did so, wondering what on earth she was going to come up with.

'Okay, you can open them.'

'Aaggh!' Aisling screamed, 'Christ on a bike, I nearly had an accident, Moira. Anyone but him!'

Moira grinned behind her Bono face mask.

'I like U2's early music when I'm doing the housework, it's so angry and full of fire it sees me finish the hoovering in next to no time,' Ro-ro announced randomly as Moira began passing the identical masks around for the group to wear.

'Ha ha, very funny,' Aisling said, leading the charge down the stairs as she peered through the round eye holes. She had to admit though it was.

THE CHAUFFEUR, WHOSE name was Ned, was well used to raucous hen nights but this was a first he thought, holding the door open. A split second ago ten female Bonos, all reeking of various perfumes and booze and wearing the sort of shoes that would put holes in your lino had piled out of the guesthouse. Now they scrambled into the back of the white stretch limo one after the other. He closed the door on their squeals over having located the mini bar before getting behind the wheel. He was grateful there was a screen separating him from them lot in the back. It was relatively peaceful here in his own little bubble. A tap on the screen before he could even turn the key in the ignition put paid to that however and he pushed the button to make it slide down.

'Ned, my man, do you happen to have any U2 with you?' the Bono he'd noticed was wearing purple knickers as she clambered into the limo asked. 'We thought it would be a great craic to play *Beautiful Day* loud and when we pull up at the lights instead of mooning people, we'll Bono them.

Sweet merciful God, it was going to be a long night, Ned thought, fishing out his U2 CD.

Chapter 18

The limousine slid expertly into the side of the kerb outside The Singing Bird shortly after midnight. Ned cocked an ear, no chance of the hens in the back having turned into pumpkins though, not given the amount of noise they were making. He looked at the flashing neon sign over the entrance to the bar and breathed a sigh of relief. This was his last stop on the pub crawl itinerary and he was more than ready to call it a night. He couldn't wait to hang up his chauffeur's cap and fix himself a warm milk to sup on before sliding in beside his Janice who'd be snoring her head off by now. The Bonos in the back had precisely an hour here and then he'd see them safely home. They'd all be feeling a little sorry for themselves in the morning he was guessing as he got out of the limo and adjusted his cap.

The tense situation on Wellington Quay was seemingly forgotten about with the prospect of karaoke here at The Singing Bird. The exclusive brick Clarence hotel on Wellington Quay was owned by Bono and The Edge. The nightclub tucked away downstairs in its depths was where the beautiful people of the city congregated after dark. The burly fella on the door had taken umbrage to the women impersonating the man who wasn't only his boss but also his personal hero and had refused them entry. He did say he'd let the one with the purple knickers in on account of her looking like a supermodel with a Bono mask on but she'd said it was one for all and all for one or something like that. The mammy and her friend had told him it was discrimination was what it was and threatened him with going to the papers but then they heard the next and final pub was The Singing Bird and there was a stage and proper microphones and everything and they'd all but thrown themselves back in the idling limousine.

Now Ned held the door open and stood back to let the clucking hens out thinking it was lucky for them they weren't famous with the paparazzi all lurking and waiting to snap them getting out of the back of the limo. They'd need to learn a little decorum if that were the case, especially the one in the purple knickers.

Aisling straightened her dress and fluffed up her veil before linking her arm through Moira's. 'I'm having a grand time, so I am, Moira. Thank you for organising this. It's brilliant being able to let my hair down.'

'You have been a bridezilla. It's good to see you relaxed.' Moira grinned, nudging Aisling before pointing out a group of lads wey-hey-heying as they walked down the street with chips, no doubt smothered in curry sauce, in hand. Aisling was sorely tempted to charge on over and help herself to a few soggy sorry excuses for a potato but she was also keen to get inside the bar and get hold of the microphone. She blew them a kiss and received a cheer but no offer of a chip and so, linking her other arm through Leila's, she dragged them toward the neon light.

The rest of the group staggered forth, Maureen and Bronagh bringing up the rear. Maureen nearly tripped on a cobblestone but Bronagh caught her before any damage could be done. 'Sure, it's a good thing we're here to keep an eye on the young ones,' she said steadying herself.

'It is indeed, Maureen,' said Bronagh, hiccupping.

The group blinked as they found themselves in a darkened, smoky bar. It was hot and crowded, and the whiff of body odour was lurking in the air-conditioning ducts. They'd all pushed their Bono masks off having decided he would be too hard to emulate on stage. Roisin shouted over the top of the woman who was murdering Whitney Houston up on the stage, 'Clearly there are a lot of frustrated wannabe pop stars in Dublin.'

'Jaysus, she'll put us all to sleep. We need something lively so we do,' Aisling yelled in Leila's ear. Leila looked at her, Aisling looked at Leila and simultaneously they shrieked, 'ABBA!' Off they tottered and a coup was held on the stage where they managed to wrestle the microphone from Whitney who received no support from the audience before requesting Mamma Mia. 'I'm the blonde one,' Leila stated for obvious reasons but Aisling pulled a face, 'Yes, but I'm the bride so I should get to choose. I want to be Agnetha for once.'

The familiar opening beats sounded and Leila consented, taking her position on the left of Aisling. The pair began to sway their hips and click their fingers. The dance floor filled as the catchy tune began in earnest and Aisling and Leila gave it their all. The only glitch in the performance was when they spun around to face each other with too much gusto and narrowly missed headbutting one another. Aside from that when the song drew to a close, they received loud applause. Aisling was all set for *Super Trouper* but to her surprise Ita had gotten in with a request and was waiting to take the stage. Aisling and Leila milked the spotlight a moment longer before reluctantly handing the microphone over.

Maureen had mooched up to the bar once her middle daughter and Leila had finished their double act. 'I'll have two pina coladas please,' she shouted across the sticky bar top to the young fella who, if she half shut her left eye, had the look of the dimply one from Westlife. He gave her a cocky smirk.

'What was that love? Two penis and lagers?'

Maureen was flummoxed, her gin and tequila-addled brain thought he'd said the word penis but that couldn't be right. Surely not. 'No,' she shook her head vehemently but didn't like the way it made her head spin. 'Two pina coladas,' She gave him the fingers inadvertently before assailing him with her rendition of the chorus of the famous song by the same name. 'And, I'd like the little umbrellas in them. The ones you get when you're on your holidays.'

Jaysus, he had a right one here, he thought, setting about making the cocktails, and what was with the cowgirl look? She was taking karaoke to another level.

'Can you do the Tom Cruise thing. You know from that film, what was it called, now?'

'Cocktail and it was before my time.'

'Oh.' Maureen was disappointed, she would have liked a show, so she would.

'He's no good, Bronagh, he can't do the Tom Cruise thing,' she said as she joined her to wait for the drinks.

'Ah, never mind,' Bronagh flapped her hand. 'This place has karaoke. I love karaoke me. Moira's done Aisling proud with tonight, it's been grand so it has. The meal was very good too.'

The dimply one shook his cannister.

'Give it more elbow into it, son,' Maureen called over and turning back to Bronagh, she agreed. 'She has and it was.'

They'd gone to a Mexican restaurant and had a lovely time tipping their heads back in the dentist chair for the tequila shots. Truth be told, neither woman would have been able to tell you whether they'd had nachos or a burrito to eat.

'Those two were very polished.' Bronagh pointed to the stage where Leila and Aisling were bowing deeply as though they were getting a standing ovation at the Royal Variety Show performance.

'They were. They knew all the dance moves and everything.' Maureen looked at the stage in time to see Aisling pass the microphone to Ita. 'I wonder what Ita will sing.'

'*Sadie the Cleaning Lady*,' Bronagh said, hiccupping and giggling at the same time. 'Because singing about doing the old scrub-a-dub-dub is as close as she'll get to actually giving it what for.'

Ita or Idle Ita as Moira was fond of calling her was not the most dedicated director of housekeeping. It was a fact, but still, out of loyalty to her old friend, Ita's mammy, Maureen stuck up for her. 'Ah, she's alright Ita. She had a hard time of it after her daddy left. She deserves a break.'

Both women were rendered silent though as Ita cleared her throat before beginning to sing. She'd chosen Dusty Springfield's *Son of a Preacher Man* and her voice started off with a wobble but built in confidence until it was soaring around the bar. It was one of those rare karaoke moments when someone gets up who can actually sing and people who'd been sitting in darkened corners nursing drinks were compelled to make their way onto the dance floor to move to her sultry sound.

'Who'd have thought it?' Bronagh said.

'I wonder if her mammy knows she can sing,' Maureen said.

'Here we are ladies.' Two creamy drinks in tall glasses were placed in front of the women. Each had a cocktail umbrella swizzle stick poking out the side, much to Maureen's delight. They sipped their drinks while listening to Ita.

'Look who's after getting up next.' Bronagh nudged Maureen to where Roisin, Moira and Nina were ready to storm the stage. 'Hard act to follow,' she lamented, looking sorrowfully into the depths of her drink. 'Glad it's them not us.'

Maureen agreed, joining in with the cheers, Ita received when she'd finished. There were calls for more, more but Roisin, Moira and Nina were already up and ready. As they erupted into a poppy dance song, Maureen spluttered, sending a fine spray of pina colada forth. 'Christ on a bike! Chance would be a fine thing where those two of mine are concerned.'

They'd picked *Like a Virgin* and were earnestly singing about being touched for the very first time.

By the time Ro-ro and Tina-Marie had gyrated their way through *Black Velvet*, Bronagh could feel the urge to croon welling up in her throat.

'Come on now, we can't let the side down, Maureen. It's our turn next so it is. Let's see what there is to choose from.'

Maureen drained her drink and told Bronagh she had to spend a penny and then she'd be over to join her. 'It was a very nice pina colada,' she said to the dimply one before tottering off. True to her word she was soon back flicking through the book of songs. It was on the second page her eyes alighted on the perfect tune and she looked at Bronagh. 'What do you think?'

Bronagh gave her the thumbs up wondering if she could sing and hold her stomach in at the same time. 'And you look the part, too,' she added.

Maureen looped her thumbs through the belt hooks on her skirt like she did at the line dancing classes and began uttering a quiet 'me, me, me, me,' to warm her voice up. She wound up coughing due to the smoky atmosphere but by the time they got the signal they were up, she was recovered.

'Jaysus, Mammy, Bronagh, you're not after getting up, are you?'

'Don't you be starting with the discrimination. You're only as old as you feel and we've a fine pair of lungs on us haven't we Bronagh?'

'We have indeed, Maureen. We've been around the block a few times, so.'

Maureen cast her a 'speak for yourself' glance unsure what that was supposed to mean before wagging her finger in her youngest child's face. 'Watch and learn how it's done.'

Moira shook her head watching her mammy step up on stage. She leaned into Roisin whose hand had flown to her mouth as she swallowed a giggle. 'And she was on at me about flashing my knickers to all and sundry about town.'

Nina's brown eyes were enormous at the sight of Mrs O'Mara with her skirt caught in the back of her knickers. 'I'll tell her.' But the song had already started and she didn't want to rain on her parade. 'Maybe she'll stay put and nobody will notice,' she added hopefully as Moira and Roisin clutched each other in fits. Staying put and doing nothing was not on Maureen's curriculum though and with due Dolly flair she began strutting around the stage to *9 To 5*. Bronagh's attempts to catch hold of her and wrest her skirt down as Maureen somehow managed to stay one step ahead of her only served to make the girls laugh harder. Even Nina had begun to giggle.

IT WAS APPROXIMATELY one fifty-three am by the time Ned dropped the remaining hens off back at O'Mara's. He'd been very obliging in taking the other girls, Leila included, home beforehand. The mammy one in the back had not stopped going on about how she thought her drink had been spiked by your dimply one on the bar because it was not in her character to make a holy show of herself. The purple knickers one who by all accounts hadn't touched a drop all night informed her mammy there was no drink spiking involved and the holy show was down to the gins, the tequilas and the cocktails her mammy had knocked back over the course of the evening. They were still bickering over it all as they tried to open the door to the guesthouse.

'Thank you, Ned, you've been a star so you have,' the bride-to-be said, making him blush by giving him a kiss on the cheek before sorting her mammy and sisters out. She pushed the door open and herded them inside telling them to keep the noise down because it was a guesthouse not a fecking...

Whatever it was he didn't catch it, and getting back in his limousine he drove off home knowing it would be a very long time before his U2 CD saw the light of day again.

Chapter 19

Noreen

Noreen tapped the side of the sieve and a sprinkle of icing sugar rained down on the Victoria sponge cake like snow. She stood back to admire her handiwork satisfied with the end result. It had become her signature cake around the village over the years. If ever there was a party, birthday or funeral and a cake was needed, she was enlisted to make one of her famous deep sponges. The baking of it never ceased to be bittersweet for the memories it evoked but memories were part of what made us who we were, Noreen always thought. You had to take the bad in order to have the good and as such there was no point in ignoring them. This sponge with its homemade jam, something she had time for now she no longer ran the shop, and fresh cream filling was intended for Father Peter. She wanted his advice as to what she should do about Emer and didn't like to appear at the rectory empty handed. She knew Father Peter, a portly man with a penchant for anything sweet, like her Malachy, could never resist her sponge cake, and as such she'd have his undivided attention. Noreen untied her apron and went to tidy herself up.

With her headscarf knotted beneath her chin to stop her hair from turning into a bird's nest in the gusty breeze, she set off. It was a short walk through the village to the church at its edge. She was carrying the cake in her trusty container. She'd bought it years ago when Rosamunde had begun dabbling in Tupperware parties, balking at the price of it but Rosamunde had convinced her it would be an investment. It had been too, she'd be lost without it now. She spied Maisie Donovan's cocker spaniel, Timmy, nosing around outside the butchers and held her container a little tighter. She didn't trust the animal one little bit and had threatened Maisie with a phone call to the powers that be more than once. Sure, she'd once watched the crafty dog leap around the legs of Mrs Sweeney outside that very butchers. The poor woman, nervy at the best of times, had dropped the sausages she'd bought for her and Mr Sweeney's dinner and the cocker spaniel had absconded with them, tail wagging all the way.

She shooed Timmy away as she passed by him and said hello to Mr Farrell, who told her he was off for a warming bowl of stew in Murphy's. Pint of ale more like, she'd thought, crossing over the stone bridge and hearing the stream babbling beneath it. The wind was cutting right through her today and she hoped Father Peter was in the rectory house and not the draughty old church.

The church, she saw, peering around the door and inhaling its familiar smell of pungent incense was deserted and she followed the path around to the house, noticing the hydrangeas had been cut back for the winter months. Father Peter, Father Jim and Father Thomas all lived here in the rectory and the pruned flowering shrubs would be down to Father Thomas. It was he who had the green fingers. Father Jim and Father Thomas would be out visiting the housebound of the parish as was their custom on a Thursday, which was why she was hoping to catch Father Peter for a quiet word. She placed her container down on the step before rapping on the door, feeling the tug in her back as she bent to retrieve it.

'Noreen, are you alright?' Father Peter swung the door open in time to see her grimacing as she righted herself. 'Here let me take that for you.' He relieved her of the Tupperware, his eyes lighting up as he guessed at what might be inside.

'It's age, Father Peter, nothing more.'

'Ah yes, it brings its aches and pains to be sure but how does the saying go?'

'Do not resent growing old, many are denied the privilege.'

'Truer words never spoken. Now then, come in out of the cold.'

Noreen did so and followed the priest down the shadowy hallway with its worn runner through to the kitchen where the old Aga was ticking over and keeping the room cheerful. The scent of toast hung on the air along with something else. She spied a jar with sprigs of thyme in it and realised that was the underlying smell. Beyond the back door, Noreen knew, was a well-tended garden with a raised bed of herbs and a fruitful vegetable patch. If she were to pop her head out the door, she knew she'd find parsnips, swedes, leeks and Brussel sprouts – Father Jim's penchant for the latter was well known and his reputation preceded him in the confessional box. Father Thomas kept his fellow priests well fed from his efforts in the garden. Given the priests looked after themselves, the place was kept very respectably Noreen thought, pulling out a chair and sitting down at Father Peter's bidding, noting the scrubbed table and clear worktop as she did so. They were house-proud men.

'I shall make us a cup of tea to have with what I hope I'll find in here.' He set the container down on the table at which Noreen sat.

'It's one of my Victoria sponges, Father, with fresh cream and homemade jam.'

Father Peter's eyes gleamed greedily as she'd known they would. 'Well this is a good day, a good day indeed, but to what do I owe the pleasure?'

'It's advice I'm after, Father.'

'Well now, Noreen, it has to be said I give my wisest opinions on a full stomach.' He retrieved two side plates and a knife. 'If you could do the honours while I tend to the tea that would be grand.'

'Certainly, Father.'

He nodded and set about making a pot of tea.

Noreen had placed a sliver of cake in front of herself and a large triangle for Father Jim by the time he'd set the tea things on the table. He poured them both a cup of the steaming brew before murmuring a very quick grace, smacking his lips, and tucking in.

Noreen hadn't much of an appetite but managed to fork up the best part of her cake so the priest didn't feel he was eating alone. He made short work of the sponge and in no time was pushing his chair back. He wiped his mouth with a paper napkin, missing the blob of cream on the tip of his nose. Noreen didn't like to say anything and fixed her eyes on her china cup and saucer instead.

'Now then, Noreen, let me tell you, if you were to enter that sponge of yours in a cake competition, I've no doubt it would take first place. An unexpected and most enjoyable treat on a cold winter's afternoon. Thank you.'

Noreen smiled acknowledging his praise.

'So, why don't you tell me what it is troubling you.' He clasped his hands resting them on his lap as he leaned back, satiated, in his chair.

'I've a family wedding to attend in a few weeks in Dublin and my niece who I've not spoken to after she wronged myself and my dear departed Malachy thirty years ago will be there. My sister, Rosamunde's after ringing me and telling me it's time to put old grievances aside. She wants me to find forgiveness in my heart for what her daughter did to Malachy and myself. Part of me would like very much to do this because she was like a daughter to us and I miss her, but I'm not sure I can.'

'Why don't you start at the beginning and tell me what happened all those years ago.'

Noreen finished her tea and setting it back in the saucer took a deep breath finding, herself back in 1970.

Chapter 20
1970

'This came this morning, Noreen. Read it.' Rosamunde flapped the envelope under her sister's nose. The shop was blessedly quiet because Noreen had seen from the look on her sister's face when she burst through the door she was in a state. Malachy was out and she couldn't very well close up in order to hear whatever it was in this letter that had her sister all worked up. And she certainly didn't want their customers knowing their family's private business. She glanced toward the door, willing it to stay shut for the time being, before taking the envelope from Rosamunde. She put the glasses, hanging on a chain around her neck these days, on and pulled the letter from the envelope. She recognised the handwriting instantly – it was Emer's – and her eyes scanned the page, reading quickly. As she drew near the end, her lips tightened; she could see why Rosamunde was upset.

Emer had completed a bookkeeping course in Cork after leaving school and it hadn't been long after, she'd headed for Dublin. Her new qualification had secured her a position in a furniture factory's office and she'd lodged with a group of girls she'd gotten friendly with while studying in town, all keen for a taste of capital city life. At first, she'd written regularly and had come home once a month, full of news of what life like was like in the big smoke. Noreen and Malachy had counted down the days between those visits, worrying in between times she was burning the candle at both ends, but comforting one another with the fact they knew she was happy and living life to the full. Slowly though, the letters had become fewer and the visits non-existent apart from holidays and birthdays. Independence was all part of growing up, Malachy had said, and she'd agreed with him but it didn't stop her missing Emer and was she *that* busy she couldn't write a little more often.

Noreen hadn't confided in anyone but Malachy to being a little hurt when her niece got engaged to Phelan Daly without breathing a word to her of it being on the cards. His family owned the furniture business where she worked. Emer had mentioned in passing, on a rare visit home, she'd been stepping out with the boss's son but there'd been no talk of it being serious. She hadn't even brought him home to meet the family. It had stung a little, hearing the news her precious niece was engaged to a veritable stranger via a quickly scrawled letter landing on the mat inside the front door of the shop on a Wednesday morning.

And now this. She folded the letter up and tucked it back inside the envelope before handing it back to her sister. 'Poor Emer, a broken engagement and no job as a result.' Her heart went out to her niece even as she wondered why she'd had to hear this news from Rosamunde who clearly didn't know what to do about the situation her daughter found herself in. 'She doesn't say what happened though does she? Only that her fiancé and her have parted ways which means she feels she can no longer work at the factory and she's been living off her savings this past month as finding a new job is proving a challenge.'

'Yes, but she won't be able to do that much longer. To be honest, Noreen, I'm surprised she has any savings. You know how money always burned a hole in her pocket. If she can't find work then she'll have to come home,' Rosamunde said, stuffing the envelope in the pocket of her cardigan before wringing her hands. 'But what will she do here? Sure, it's why she left in the first place. There's not much in the way of prospects for a young person in Claredoncally and around abouts.'

'There's always Cork.' Noreen had felt she should have applied for work in town when she finished her course. It was much closer to home and if it was city life she was after wanting to try, Cork was every bit as much a city as Dublin, though granted a little smaller.

'There is but I think she needs to be home with her family in order to get over all the upset with Phelan, and sure the bus to town is slower than a horse and cart. It would take her well over an hour to get in and out every day. You know how she hated it when she was studying. No, I was thinking something closer to home.'

Ah, *now* Noreen could see what had brought her sister steaming over to the shop. She'd never been very subtle. She sighed, her words coming out in an exasperated hiss, 'Rosamunde, why don't you say what it is you came to say?'

Rosamunde licked her lips and eyed her sister speculatively for a moment. 'Alright then. You always were straight to the point, Noreen. Would you see your way to giving Emer a job here at the shop, until she can get herself on her feet again?'

It was as she'd thought. 'I don't know, Rosamunde. I don't think there'd be enough work here to keep her busy.'

'Noreen, please, she needs your help.'

It was all she'd ever wanted; to be needed the way a child needs her mammy and Emer was the closest thing to a daughter she was ever going to have. Of course, she wanted to keep her close, she would like nothing more than to work alongside her but it was pointless if all they'd be doing was twiddling their thumbs. 'I'll talk it over with Malachy.'

'Bless you, Noreen, you're one in a million so you are.'

One month later...

'Emer, you'll rub a hole in the glass if you polish that window any harder,' Noreen said, opening the till. 'I'm going to finish up for the day. Put your rag away and get yourself off home.'

'Right-ho, Aunty Nono,' Emer called back cheerfully, finally satisfied she had the panes gleaming. She dropped the cloth back in the bucket and returned it to the cupboard under the stairs. Next, she went to take her shop coat off, but first things first, she pulled the crumpled pound note from her pocket and stuffed it into her bag hanging on the hook on the door. It separated the shop from the stairs leading to the living quarters upstairs. Then she took her coat off, glad to see the back of the ugly old thing as she hung it in place of her bag. She was off to the cinema tonight with her friend, Delia, and had been short thanks to the dress she'd treated herself to with last week's wages. Now she'd be able to wear her new dress, have dinner in the cafe Delia had suggested, *and* go to the cinema. Sure, she was only after taking what was her due anyway. She worked hard, her arm was aching from polishing the windows so it was, and received a pittance in return. Yes, it was only fair she justified, flicking her hair out from under jacket collar before wandering back into the shop to turn the sign from open to closed as had become her habit on her way out each evening.

'Goodnight, Aunty Nono, Uncle Malachy, see you tomorrow.'

Malachy grunted his goodbye from where he was sitting on a stool pricing a late delivery of tinned fruit.

'Have a good evening, Emer,' Noreen called, smiling back at her niece, pleased to note the colour was beginning to return to her cheeks now she was away from the city with all its pollution and grime. Fresh air was a tonic for most things, a broken heart included, she thought as the door banged shut behind their newest employee.

She began to tally up the day's takings counting silently as she did the arithmetic that had become second nature to her over the years. For the second time that month though it didn't add up. She prided herself on being accurate when it came to her dealings with their customers and Emer, well, Emer was a qualified bookkeeper. She knew her figures right enough. She frowned and looked down the aisle at Malachy. He needed reading glasses but refused to admit this was the case. Was he after giving out too much change? She'd have to broach the topic carefully with him, he could be a sensitive soul. She made her mind up to talk to him and nudging the till shut with her hip she put the coins and notes in the bag. They kept their money bag in the sideboard drawer with Malachy taking the week's earnings to the bank each Friday. 'I'll go and put the dinner on,' she called over to her husband. He was a pussycat on a full stomach.

Three months later...

'Where's our Emer?' Rosamunde asked Noreen one afternoon as she picked up a tin of baked beans and put them in her basket. 'They'll go nicely with our sausages tonight.' She put another tin in for good measure. The boys had hollow legs on them these days and she debated a third tin but decided no, they'd have to fill their boots with slices of bread on the side.

'It's Friday, she's gone into town to do the banking.'

'It was very good of Malachy to teach her to drive. Terry wouldn't have had the patience.'

'He didn't mind. She picked it up easily by all accounts and Malachy wanted to give her a sense of responsibility by getting her to do the banking and collect the odd order. She's qualified in bookkeeping and the like so it must bore her silly stacking shelves and serving customers all day.'

'She's seems happy enough to me. It's working out well then? Having Emer here.'

'It is.' Noreen had to admit it was, they'd be lost without her now. 'I was worried we mightn't find enough for her to do but business is brisk. People always need their milk and bread and other essentials. Her being here means Malachy and I can take things a little easier, too.' They were enjoying the opportunity Emer's presence afforded them to take more breaks, she'd even found Malachy upstairs with his feet up and the paper spread out in front of him the other day! It wasn't only

Malachy who was making the most of not being needed on the shop floor continuously. She'd slipped away and had her hair set the other day and found time for a cup of tea with her old friend, Kathleen, at Alma's. Mind you, she'd nearly broken a tooth on her currant bun, rock hard so they were. She'd told Alma in no uncertain terms, if she wanted to keep her customers, she needed to up her game.

Rosamunde hesitated in that way of hers which told Noreen she had something weighing on her chest.

'Come on then, Rosamunde, I can see you've not called in for the baked beans alone. Out with it.'

Her younger sister looked shifty as she dug deep for the words she was after. She cleared her throat. 'I, erm, I was wondering what you're paying Emer, that's all.'

'The going rate, why?' Noreen was put out by Rosamunde implying they were making the most of their niece being family and employing her on slave wages.

'Oh, don't get snippy, Noreen. I know you're more than fair with her. But she's forever coming home with new things that to my mind should be beyond her means.'

Noreen smoothed her ruffled feathers before speaking. 'Sure, she's young, isn't she? The young are apt to be spendthrifts.' It wasn't necessarily true. She hadn't been, she'd been a diligent saver from the moment she'd picked up her first brown envelope from the wages clerk at the fish factory but then she'd had something to save for, a shared dream with Malachy. It was neither here nor there, times were different now and Emer was entitled to enjoy herself. She worked hard and she'd obviously been through a lot with that fickle Phelan fellow in Dublin. Not that she'd ever spoken about it. She'd made it clear when

Noreen had tried to broach the subject to find out what had gone wrong, it was a topic she didn't wish to talk about. Fair enough, Noreen had thought. Some things were too painful to speak of and so she'd left it, figuring Emer was healing her heart in her own way.

'Hmm,' Rosamunde mumbled, but didn't look satisfied. 'She's more clothes than she knows what to do with these days and it's not as if she needs them for work. She's gotten very off-hand with me lately too because when I asked her about it, she told me it was none of my business. I told her it was my business while she was under my roof and she said something about not being under it for much longer before slamming her bedroom door. Terry was livid, said she'd have it hanging off the hinges with that sort of behaviour.'

Noreen frowned unable to picture the scene her sister had painted. 'That doesn't sound like Emer. I've never heard her say a cross word.'

Rosamunde heaved her laden basket onto the counter. 'Oh, you've always been blind to her faults, Noreen. You and Malachy both. She's a side to her at times that one. Nobody's perfect you know. She's a long way to fall from the pedestal you have her on,' Rosamunde said, before shaking her head in a manner which made Noreen feel spiky with irritation and her words niggled Noreen for a long while after she'd left.

Chapter 21

'Can I interrupt you there, Noreen?' Father Peter said. 'I can see it's distressing you talking about this and sure, everybody knows there's no trouble so great or grave that cannot be much diminished by a cup of tea.' He took the cosy off the pot and poured another strong brew for her, leaving her to help herself to the milk and sugar. She didn't normally take sugar but today she put a teaspoon in. The sugar would help calm the anxiety raking over the past had wrought.

'Another slice of your delicious cake?' Father Peter held the knife poised over the sponge hopefully.

'No thank you, Father, but sure, help yourself. I made it to be enjoyed.'

'And that it will be, Noreen, that it will be,' he muttered, slicing into it.

She sipped her tea allowing the hot, sweet liquid to settle her nerves while he slid a generous wedge onto his plate and began to wolf it down with as much gusto as he had the first piece. This time when he'd finished and wiped his mouth he managed, to Noreen's relief, to remove the cream from his nose.

'Now then, Noreen, you're looking much more composed,' Father Peter said, pushing the plate away from him, his clasped hands resting around a middle clearly straining against his shirt. 'Are you ready to carry on?'

'I am, thank you, Father.'

1970

It was a day of rainbows when Noreen ventured into Cork. There was a sale on in Roches Stores there on Patrick Street and as she made her way toward the building with its grand copper-covered dome, she could see the line of eager shoppers waiting for the doors to open. She and Malachy had left it to Emer to open the shop in order to pootle into the city at an ungodly hour of the morning. Malachy was going to the grocery wholesalers while she fought the crowd in the women's clothing department here at Roches. They'd arranged to meet outside the store's main door for midday in order to go and treat themselves to a spot of lunch. The thought of standing around outside the frontage like so many youngsters did on a Friday evening, waiting to meet their date made her smile. At least her stomach wouldn't be all of a flutter wondering whether he'd show up or she'd find herself stood up and sloping off home on the bus. He'd always been a reliable sort, her Malachy.

Noreen reached the store and tagged onto the end of the chattering queue. There was a sense of excitement in the air at the thought of the glorious bargains about to be found inside and she crossed her fingers in the pocket of her smart, going into town jacket hoping she'd be able to find what it was she'd come for. It wasn't herself she was after shopping for today. No, it was Emer. She'd seen the look of yearning in her niece's eye the day Mrs Darby had breezed unexpectedly into their shop.

Mrs Darby was a mythical creature who lived in the big house halfway between their village and the next town. She spoke with a plum wedged firmly in her lipsticked mouth and was hardly ever seen on the streets of Claredoncally, preferring to do her shopping in town. So, when her sleek grey, automobile pulled up on the main street, Maisie Donovan had burst through the door of Grady's Convenience Store full of this breaking news. Emer had gone to the window, pressing her nose to it as she peered down the street before declaring excitedly that the glamorous vision wrapped in a royal blue, belted wrap coat and matching hat was heading toward their shop. Noreen had fluffed her hair and straightened her shop coat before standing to attention as though she were about to greet the Queen behind the counter.

Indeed, the door had jangled a moment later and the lady herself had swept into the store bringing with her a cloud of cloying perfume. Noreen had wanted to hiss at Maisie to close her great big gawping mouth because she looked like the village idiot which was all well and good for her but there was no need to make them all look bumpkins. She was out of earshot though, lurking alongside the packets of digestive biscuits she'd been wondering whether to have with her morning tea and so Noreen had to bite her tongue. Emer had leaped to attention and was fawning all over the elegant apparition asking what she could fetch for her. She wouldn't be able to complain the service at Grady's wasn't up to speed Noreen had thought proudly as she watched her niece scurry toward her in order to fetch the newspaper which Mrs Darby was bemoaning had not arrived at Briar House that morning. It meant Mr Darby's day had not gotten off to a good start, she informed Emer tightly.

Noreen handed the correct change to Emer, observing her press it into Mrs Darby's gloved hand. She'd half thought her niece might curtsey as she received a nod by way of thank you. Then, leaving nothing but her expensive scent in her wake, Mrs Darby was gone. They all stood in reverent silence for a good few minutes until Emer, who'd resumed her position at the window, announced the car had slipped away from the main street. Their shoulders relaxed and business resumed as normal. Maisie decided she deserved a digestive with her tea and she'd push the boat out and buy a packet of the chocolate covered biscuits. It wasn't every day there was this much excitement in Claredoncally.

Noreen had been driven demented all afternoon listening to Emer drone on and on about what perfume Mrs Darby had been wearing. Did she think it was Dior or Guerlain? It was definitely French, her niece informed her. 'Did you see her coat, Aunty Nono?' It wasn't as if she could have missed it, Noreen thought, as Emer gushed further. 'I bet you it was from Paris. I heard she goes to the fashion shows there and buys her clothes direct from the designers. That's why she looks like a film star.' Her eyes were alight and her chin was resting on her cupped hands. She was leaning on the counter in a manner that would have Malachy telling her to stand up straight because the staff at Grady's Convenience Store didn't slouch, if he were to spot her. Noreen didn't ask how her niece knew all this about Mrs Darby's wardrobe but was guessing it was fodder for village gossip. She'd been unable to stop herself from rolling her eyes as Emer pondered aloud as to what the interior of Briar House was like.

'Sure, Emer,' she'd said. 'It's only a house. We've all got to live somewhere and the bigger the house the more cleaning there is to be done.'

Emer was undeterred. 'I bet it's very grand with priceless art and antiques everywhere. Imagine having someone to cook for you and someone to clean for you, Aunty Nono. Imagine if all you had to do was click your fingers and someone would come running.'

'I wouldn't like it,' Noreen stated, her niece's enthusiasm for the Darbys' ostentatious lifestyle was making her cringe. She paused in her clicking of the price gun, leaving the remaining jars of coffee she'd been unpacking in the box for a moment. 'No, it wouldn't be for me to have a stranger living in my home privy to all our private business. And sure, why does anyone need more rooms than they can ever use?'

But Emer hadn't wanted to hear about practical things; she wanted to daydream about impractical things such as big houses full of servants, French perfume, and coats the latest fashion in Paris.

'There's no point getting ideas of grandeur, Emer. It only makes you hanker for things you can't have and there's no happiness to be found in doing so,' Noreen had said, trying to snap her niece out of it. Her words were wise but still, she'd thought, there was no harm in the girl having a smart new coat and while Roches Stores might not be the Paris catwalk, she was sure she'd find a style similar to Mrs Darby's collared, wrap coat. Royal blue would look well on Emer, and she and Malachy would be lost without her these days. It would be nice to acknowledge how indispensable they found her with a thank you gift. The bottom line though, Noreen knew, was she wanted to see her face light up when she pulled the coat from the bag and it was for this reason, she was currently listening in on a most interesting tale the woman in front of her was after telling her friend as she waited for Roches to open their doors.

She was about to find out what had happened to Bridie at the dance last Friday night when she'd felt a tap on her shoulder. She swung around to see a face she recognised but couldn't quite place. The girl, around Emer's age, registered her confusion and explained. 'Hello, Mrs Grady, I'm Angela. We met a while ago when I came home with Emer for a weekend. She brought me by your shop to say hello. Emer and I shared a room in Dublin.'

Ah yes, the penny dropped, she'd been pleased to meet the girl and have a peek through the window into what Emer's life in Dublin was like. 'Angela, yes of course. It's lovely to see you again. How're you?'

'I'm grand, thanks.'

'Are you working here in town these days?' she asked, noting the girl's smart blouse and skirt. She had a name badge pinned to her chest and her hair was pulled back in a tidy ponytail.

'I am, yes. I've a job at the Bank of Ireland. I transferred from Dublin not long after Emer left.' Her expression closed a little. 'Things were a little awkward after everything that happened. I'm pleased I ran into you because I've wondered how she's doing?'

Noreen was puzzled, the girl was being very cryptic. 'Have you not been in touch with her yourself then?' Perhaps the pair had had a falling out. It couldn't have been easy sharing a poky bedroom. You'd be forever stepping on one another's toes.

Angela wouldn't meet her eye. 'No, I haven't.'

Something had definitely gone on, Noreen thought, but it wasn't any of her business. 'Well, I for one think leaving Dublin and having a fresh start has been the best thing for her. She's working for me and Mr Grady at the shop now and living back with her mammy and da for the time being.'

Angela looked startled by this news.

Noreen couldn't help herself. 'Sure, why don't you phone her. You two were thick as thieves weren't you.'

Angela blanched at Noreen's terminology and she flapped her hand dismissively, her manner telling Noreen she was keen to be on her way. 'Ah, no, tell her I was asking after her would you? I'm glad things are working out.'

'They are. She had a lucky escape when that Phelan one broke off their engagement.' Noreen could never keep the righteousness from her voice when she breathed that man's name. It raised her ire to think of him casting her beautiful niece aside the way he had and it was a good job he'd never shown his face in Claredoncally.

Angela's cheeks burned hot with two red blotches and her words tumbled out before she could stop them. 'Well, he hardly had any choice not after what Emer did. I'm sorry, Mrs Grady, but I don't think that's a fair comment.'

Noreen was taken aback by the girl's strong reaction. Her pulse quickened the way it always did when she knew things could go one of two ways. She could leave the conversation there and pretend she'd never met up with Angela. She could carry on happily about her business or, she could push further and find out something instinct was telling her she wouldn't want to hear. She and Rosamunde had assumed Phelan had gotten cold feet and Emer had never given them reason to think otherwise but here was Angela alluding to Emer being the one at fault. She couldn't help herself, the plaster had to be ripped off now. 'And what do you mean by that?'

'Nothing.' Angela wished she'd kept her mouth shut. 'I shouldn't have said anything. It's just, well it's not fair on Phelan you thinking he's faithless. I'd best be on my way or I'll be late.' She made to walk away.

Noreen put her hand on Angela's forearm, stopping her. 'Please, Angela, will you tell me what Emer did?'

Angela hesitated. There was a pleading look on Mrs Grady's face. She didn't know why she was so surprised Emer hadn't told her family the truth of what had happened with Phelan. She'd proven she wasn't to be trusted when she left Dublin in disgrace. Sure, she'd left her in the lurch having to cover her share of the rent, upping and leaving without a word of notice the way she did. Angela was a firm believer in second chances though, and she'd hoped Emer might have changed her ways. She'd hoped this because, despite her sneaky, dishonest streak, she was also brilliant fun and they'd had lots of laughs together in Dublin. She missed her old friend but not enough to pick up where they'd left off, besides which, she had a feeling Emer wouldn't thank her for visiting her in Claredoncally.

Angela hadn't a clue why she'd done what she'd done either, because if she was short of money, she'd only had to ask and Phelan would have helped her. Come to that she would have helped her. But she'd never even hinted at having money problems. She'd simply helped herself to what wasn't hers and when she got caught, she'd been tearful and apologetic, pleading with

Phelan not to break things off. She'd only taken the extra she was due, she'd cried. She worked hard and deserved more than the paltry sum she was paid at the end of each week. Angela had heard all of this from where she was perched on the edge of her bed in their room. She'd stared unseeingly at the wallpaper with its faded flowers and patch of damp in the corner, biting her thumbnail in disbelief as Emer's and Phelan's voices carried up the stairs from the hallway where they stood. He'd only raised his voice the once, when Emer refused to give him back the ring he'd proposed to her with. 'It belonged to my grandmother and you're not taking that from me too!' he'd shouted, and Angela had blanched picturing the scene below. The last thing she heard him say before the door banged shut behind him was, 'You're not the girl I thought you were.'

Emer had refused to talk to her about what had transpired but Angela had seen the white band on her finger, left behind by the ring. The story of Emer thieving from her employers, her fiancé's parents no less, had filtered through their circle of friends and when she found herself ostracised, she'd packed her bags. Angela had arrived home from work to a note Emer had scrawled to say she couldn't afford to stay in Dublin and had gone back to Claredoncally to stay with family.

'Are you sure you want to know?' she asked Mrs Grady. She'd only met Emer's aunt and uncle the once but she'd seen the way they fussed over their niece and their eagerness to meet her friend. They were good people and if Emer was up to her old tricks then her poor aunt deserved to know what she was capable of, especially as she was working for her in their shop these days. She chewed her bottom lip, still uncertain she wanted to be the one to tell the sorry tale.

Noreen bobbed her head, willing the girl to spit it out whatever it was. Sure, she was beginning to wonder from the drama of it all if it was murder Emer was after committing.

'Alright then. I'm sorry, Mrs Grady, but Emer was fiddling the books at the factory. Stealing to put it plainly. She was lucky the family didn't press charges when she got caught out, but you can see why Phelan had to break their engagement off. Even if he could have found a way to get past what she'd done, his family couldn't. He was heartbroken.' Her face flashed with sympathy for Emer's ex-fiancé. Noreen stood there feeling a little other worldly and something else. It took her a moment to work out what it was. Foolish, that was how she felt. A naïve and foolish woman. She was relieved when Angela announced, 'I've got to get back to work. I thought you should know in case, well, I thought you should know.'

In case a leopard didn't change its spots, Noreen finished silently for her. She couldn't muster up any words to say to Angela and as the girl shifted from foot to foot waiting for, well, Noreen wasn't sure what exactly she was waiting for because what could she say by way of response? After a painfully eked out silence she took her cue and with an apologetic goodbye, strode off down the street. Noreen watched her, unsure if the bile that had risen in her throat was at the thought of her niece being no better than a common criminal, or whether it was because of her own stupidity in not having pressed her further. She should have kept at her until she told the truth of what had happened between her and Phelan. She should have known something wasn't right. A numbness began to creep through her limbs and she forced herself to move before it rendered her frozen to the spot.

The doors to the store had opened and the line was finally snaking inside the building but Noreen left her place in the queue and headed for the AIB Bank where she and Malachy held their account, the bewilderment Rosamunde had expressed over the money Emer seemed to be splashing about foremost in her mind. The throwaway comment, her sister had made as to Noreen and Malachy holding Emer up to be something she was not played over in her mind. They'd trusted Emer week after week with their takings. When had either of them last thought to check a bank statement? She'd do so now, she thought, pushing open the doors and joining the handful of people waiting to attend to their business. She stared at the man in front of her. He was wearing a brown suit and she didn't notice the fluffy lint stuck to it as she normally would, tutting to herself she'd never let Malachy leave the house like that. She didn't disapprove over the creased trousers either as she prayed silently she wouldn't find what the sick feeling now settled in her stomach was telling her she'd find when she looked into things.

'SHE'D BEEN HELPING herself the whole time. Malachy and I were taken for gullible fools, Father.' Noreen wrung her hands as she finished her tale, her throat feeling heavy with the effort to keep the tears at bay. Even now, so many years later, the abuse of trust wounded her to her core.

'No, Noreen.' Father Peter shook his head. 'Big hearted and trusting was what you and Malachy were.'

Noreen looked at Father Peter's kindly face, drawing strength from it. 'You know it wasn't the stealing that hurt the most. It wasn't even the awful words Emer hurled at us before she left.' She shivered recalling how, when confronted, Emer had at first denied any wrongdoing. It was only when Noreen waved the statement and the book, the indisputable proof of glaring and unexplainable discrepancies, she'd begun to apologise. She'd wanted a few nice things, to treat herself, was that so bad? She was sorry, she'd pleaded. Malachy had stood by Noreen's side, his expression set in stone, and when Emer saw her apology wasn't going to be accepted with the understanding she felt was her due, she'd lashed out.

Noreen had flinched as though physically slapped when Emer threw at them she'd only taken what was her due, what she was worth, and then a nastiness had seeped in. 'You suffocated me with your neediness, did you know that?' Her eyes were as mean as her words. Malachy had spoken then, his voice hard as steel as he told her to leave the shop and not to come back. There was a look of disbelief on Emer's face and her gaze swung to Noreen, who even then wanted to take her niece in her arms and tell her all was forgiven. She stood firm by Malachy's side though, as was her duty, and Emer slammed out of the shop leaving her and Malachy to stand in hollow silence. Noreen would never forget the look on her husband's face when he at last turned to her and said, 'Well, that's that.' He never spoke of Emer again.

'What cut the deepest, Father,' Noreen said, blinking away the images from the past, 'was the way the light went out in Malachy's eyes that day.'

Chapter 22

Noreen couldn't believe a week had passed since she'd been at Alma's Tea Shop. Her days didn't normally race by, they were more inclined to meander past like a lazy stream but she'd been lost in her memories and hours had disappeared at a time. Yes indeed, time had gotten away from her as she'd lingered in the past because here she was, back at the tea shop once more. She greeted Kathleen, Margaret and Agnes, who were already there knitting like the clappers. On a plate in front of each of them was a currant bun sliced in two with a miserly spread of butter, with a pot of tea in the centre of the table. Alma was clattering away behind the counter arranging the food cabinet for what she no doubt hoped would be the lunchtime rush. Noreen pulled a chair out and sat herself down next to Margaret.

'Currant bun, Noreen?' Alma called over.

'No, thank you, but a cup and saucer would be grand.' She was cutting back on extras such as currant buns between now and her trip to Dublin. It wasn't exactly a hardship when it came to Alma's offerings. The slice of cream cake visiting Father Peter the other day was eaten out of necessity to be polite but there was no risk of offending her three old friends if she didn't partake of a currant bun. Right now though, there was an acrid odour in the air hinting at a disaster in the kitchen. 'What's that awful stink, Alma?' Her nose wrinkled.

'I was after burning the scones on account of a phone call from my daughter. I forgot all about them. The smell's murder to get rid of and it's too cold to have the place airing out.' She waved the cloth she held in her hand. 'You don't notice it after a while.'

'That's true enough,' Kathleen said, looking up from her knitting. 'Although if my coat reeks of burnt scones, it's you I'll be sending the dry cleaning bill to.'

'Ah sure, hang it in on the washing line for half an hour when you get home. Give it a good airing and it'll be good as new. There's not enough money in a pot of tea and a currant bun for the likes of the drycleaners.'

Kathleen's mouth twitched, she did so enjoy getting a rise out of Alma.

'Stop baiting her, Kathleen, would you?' Agnes paused in her lightning-fast stitches.

She could knit with her eyes closed, Noreen thought, eyeing her needles, from beneath which the beginnings of a mustard sweater were emerging.

'You know what she's like. She'll refuse to top the pot up unless we pay for another brew. How're you, Noreen?' Agnes asked, turning her wily blue eyes on her friend.

Noreen would have liked to say she was grand, but she wasn't, and she'd known these three women too long to bother pretending. She felt as though she had the weight of the world on her shoulders despite her visit to Father Peter, though she'd come away clearer in her mind as to what the right thing to do as a good Catholic woman was where Emer was concerned. This was all well and good, but to take the first step towards forgiveness at the wedding was not going to be an easy thing to do. Would the proverbial olive branch withstand the amount of water that had gone under their bridge? 'I'm right enough, thank you, Aggie.' That about summed it up she thought, opening her knitting bag and setting her things down on the table. She'd a new project to be starting and she was eager to cast the cheerful red wool on. Perhaps the bright colour would lift her mood.

'Did you find an outfit for your grand niece's wedding?' Margaret asked.

Margaret had seen her waiting at the bus stop the day she'd tripped into town to go shopping. 'I did. I went to Debenhams and decided on a green dress with three quarter sleeves, given it's winter, and a matching jacket. It's very smart.'

'And you've the shoes, bag and hat too, I hope?' Agnes chirped, looking at her currant bun. 'Dust dry, so it is.' She shook her head.

'I have, indeed.'

'You'll have to give us a fashion show, Noreen,' Kathleen said.

Noreen nodded, having no intention of doing anything of the sort as she deftly looped the wool over her needles.

'And what of a present?' Margaret inquired, pausing in her clacking to sip at her tea.

'I did well there. I chose a Waterford Crystal vase, one of their lace patterns. It's lovely so it is.'

There was a low hum of 'ooh, lucky girl' along with 'that would have set you back a pretty penny.'. It was interrupted by Alma placing a cup and saucer down in front of Noreen with more of a clatter than was necessary.

'I see, so let me get this straight. There's money for Waterford Crystal vases and the like but not a penny spare for a currant bun,' Alma muttered.

'Oh, go on with you if it means you'll leave me in peace to enjoy my tea, I'll have one of your buns. No butter mind, Alma, and if I can't do the zip up on my dress on the day it'll be you who's to blame.'

Alma scuttled off to fetch the bun, thoroughly pleased with herself.

As it happened the vase had been generously discounted but nobody needed to know that. 'Sure, it's nice to receive something special when you embark on married life.'

She didn't recall Waterford Crystal or the like being received on her wedding day. From memory there'd been practical things for the kitchen. People didn't give extravagant gifts back then, there wasn't the money for it for one thing, and for another, people didn't expect so much.

'That was a sigh from the bottom of your boots.' Kathleen's keen eyes glanced over Noreen. 'What's up with you?'

Noreen pressed her lips together tightly for a second or two as her friend waited for her to speak. 'Ah, it's this business of Emer being at the wedding. Did I tell you Rosamunde's after ringing and telling me it's time to let bygones be bygones and a wedding is a time full of hope for the future. What was I supposed to say to that?'

The three women clucked in sympathy but it was Agnes who spoke. 'Not much you could say, Noreen, not without coming across as a bitter old woman. She put you on the spot there, alright.'

'Exactly, Aggie,' Noreen said, recalling how Rosamunde had gone on to say, in what she had thought a condescending manner given she was the younger sister, 'What better opportunity to put things right between the pair of you?' What Noreen didn't understand was why it had to be her who had to make the first move. It was Emer who was in the wrong and she'd vocalised this to her sister but Rosamunde had only tutted and said that was the problem where she and Emer were concerned. They were peas in a pod. Far too stubborn for their own good and someone had to reach out first. So, why shouldn't it be Noreen?

She'd left Father Peter's the other day having heard the same sentiment from him. She'd also realised, as she'd sat relaying the story of what had happened all those years ago, how much she missed Emer. Her leaving Claredoncally had left a gaping hole in her life and the plain truth of the matter was, Noreen was lonely. She'd come here to Alma's once a week and meet her friends, listening to them bat back and forth about their children and grandchildren. She liked to keep up with all the goings on in their lives but later, when she went home to her quiet, little house, she'd feel an emptiness. The sound of children's laughter would never bounce off this house's walls. She'd always thought she would take on the role of another grandmother to Emer's children just as she'd played the role of a second mother to her growing up. She'd missed out on knowing Emer's family. The children would all be grown and have no interest in spending time with their widowed great aunt.

'I think Rosamunde has a point,' Kathleen said, having clearly mulled over what Noreen had told them. Spying the expression on Noreen's face, she held up her hand. 'No, don't give me that gin-soaked-prune look of yours. Hear me out.'

Noreen's lips tightened once more and she knitted a frantic red row with her head tilted to one side. It was enough to show Kathleen she was listening.

'I've known you long enough to know it's a heavy burden you carry where Emer is concerned. What she did was wrong but Malachy dug his heels in when he could have asked her why she'd done it.'

Noreen made to protest he had asked and hadn't liked her answer but she closed her mouth knowing what Kathleen meant was, what lay at the root of what she'd done.

'You couldn't cross his decision but I think if you'd had a say in it all back then, you'd have patched things up with her. Malachy isn't here anymore, Noreen, and knowing him as I did, I'm telling you as one of your oldest friends he wouldn't want you to be alone. There are friends and there are family in this world of ours. We get to choose our friends but not our family and when it all boils down to the nitty-gritty, if we don't have family what do we have?'

'Hear, hear,' Alma said, placing the currant bun in front of Noreen. Noreen didn't have the energy to tell her not to be listening in on a private conversation, besides she knew she'd be wasting her breath. Alma was an eavesdropper of the highest order. The door jangled announcing a customer, and with a groan about her knees not being able for all this standing she waddled off back behind the counter.

'But how?' Noreen muttered to the trio, none of whom were knitting.

'How what?' Agnes asked.

'What do I say to her?' This was the part that was all a puzzle. Should she walk up to her niece at the reception with her hand held out and say, It's time we buried the hatchet. Or should she act as though nothing had happened and chat away to her as if she had no cares in the world.

'Tell her the truth. Tell her you want to put the past behind you,' Kathleen, who was full of wise advice this morning, said.

'She's right,' Agnes agreed, dabbing the crumbs up off her plate with her index finger. Despite her protestations there was nothing left of the bun. 'It's simple.' She popped her finger in her mouth.

Was it simple after all? Noreen pondered. Perhaps, she thought, a spark of hope for the future igniting, it wasn't too late to start over again after all.

Chapter 23

Aisling and Quinn shuffled about the floor trying to mimic the actions of Maria and Antonio Lozano who were gyrating toward one another in a manner that suggested they should get a room. The beat of the fast-paced salsa music Aisling had picked for their wedding dance was filling the studio above the shops on Dame Street. 'Do you not think it's a little over the top?' Quinn whispered to Aisling who had to resist the urge not to stomp on his foot.

'No, I don't. I think it's very romantic.'

'But we're Irish not South American.'

'Oh, so would you rather me wear a red ringlet wig and a short green dress and jig my way across the floor toward you?'

'Not at all, but we could do a swaying, slow dance sort of a thing, couldn't we?' Hope sparked in his eyes but it was doused as Aisling jeered back at him, 'Everybody has that. I don't want our wedding to be like everyone else's.'

Quinn gave up and tried to concentrate on emulating their instructors. He'd mastered a few steps at the lessons he and Aisling had done before they'd become a couple but he was by no means a natural.

Aisling eyed Maria and Antonio thinking Quinn had a point as the couple oozed sensuality and rhythm, unlike them. They were like two wooden puppets, Punch and Judy she thought huffily, with hip swivel problems. She flung her arms up in frustration and stepped back from him. 'This is hopeless,

Maria, Antonio! I can't seem to find my rhythm.' She looked down at the swingy skirt and towering heels she'd worn thinking they'd put her in the mood to salsa about, before glaring at Quinn as though it were all his fault. The look on his face told her he'd rather be anywhere but here. She fumed silently, unsure why he kept throwing cold water over all her ideas. First the table settings were over the top and now this. Well tough, she'd asked the husband and wife salsa duo to help choreograph their wedding dance and they'd agreed, although they weren't doing it out of the goodness of their hearts. They were charging like wounded bulls, not that she'd tell Quinn. Time was money and she couldn't afford for the magic not to be happening on the dance floor tonight.

Quinn rubbed his temples, he was feeling very secondhand thanks to his uncommon night on the town. His brothers had kept it clean but had been enthusiastically sliding all manner of shooters down the bar top towards him for most of the evening. Quinn had knocked them back with equal enthusiasm. It had been a good craic at the time. He hadn't been smiling when he'd woken with a banging head on Sunday morning though. Although he'd felt a little better by the time his mam had filled him and his da, who was also suffering loudly, up with a plate of bacon, eggs and beans to soak up the remains of the night before. He'd wiped his plate clean and drunk his milky tea, thanking his mam before taking himself off to ring Aisling, eager to know how her hen night had been.

Aisling was feeling surprisingly chipper given it was the morning after her hen night. She'd put it down to the big glass of water Moira had told her she should get down her when she'd gotten home. She'd filled Quinn in on the Bono masks and the limousine that had ferried them about the city in style. He'd laughed as she told him about Maureen's karaoke faux pax. His poor mammy-in-law-to-be was, by all accounts, green around the gills today, although like him her delicate state had been helped by a full Irish. Mrs Baicu, the guesthouse's weekend cook had put a good lining on the O'Mara women's stomachs after which Maureen had announced, once she'd deposited Roisin at the airport, she was going home where she'd be receiving no calls or visitors for the rest of the day. Aisling, having finished relaying the events of her evening had reminded Quinn about this, their dance lesson, and he'd groaned into the receiver. 'Can't we give it a miss tonight, Aisling?'

She'd adopted a high-pitched timbre he was coming to recognise as one meaning she wasn't to be pushed on the subject. 'No,' she'd said, 'they could not cancel because there would be a cancellation fee. The Lozanos were busy people and, as such, they might not be able to fit them in again on short notice. And,' the pitch went up several notches, 'do I need to remind you the wedding is in less than two weeks?' Quinn had decided he was best to go with the flow and hadn't argued, which was why he was here now learning a routine to perform with Ash in front of all their friends and family. Was he happy about it? No, he was not. He felt like a complete eejit for one thing and knew his brothers would never let him live the moment down. Sure, he could imagine the names they'd be coming up with, ole swivel hips and the like. He knew why she had her heart set on salsa. It was his own fault and the knowledge of this irked him even more. He'd won her over with a salsa dance in this very studio, but it had been for her eyes only. It was no good telling her he felt ridiculous though, her mind was made up. Come February the fourteenth, they'd be performing the Latin American dance in front of an audience of family and friends. He was beginning to dread the fecking wedding.

'Aisling, Quinn,' Maria said, in a manner managing to be both sultry and smooth, which always made Aisling think of Galaxy chocolate. 'You are not feeling the music in here.' She put her hand on her breast and Aisling elbowed Quinn. 'Remember, you're nearly a married man.'

'Salsa,' Antonio stated passionately, 'connects you with others. It is sexy and energetic. We come together to be our true selves and to be in the moment. Salsa is magic.'

'Jaysus, feck, he knows that little speech off by heart,' Quinn muttered, receiving a sharp elbow once more.

And on the count of three, away they went again. It was going to be a long night, thought Quinn as he stuck his bottom out and quickstepped toward Aisling.

Chapter 24

A isling let Moira daub the deep conditioning treatment on her head. She'd asked her sister to give her a facial but she was going the whole hog massaging the conditioner into her scalp. She closed her eyes, feeling her shoulders relax. 'You're pretty good at this.'

'Thank you,' Moira said, piling her sister's hair on top of her head before disappearing into the kitchen. 'I need the cling film.'

'Why?'

She returned with the box and pulled a length from it before ripping it off the serrated edge. 'I'm going to wrap it around your head so it keeps your scalp warm, it makes the treatment more effective.'

'Will you leave me holes to breath?' Aisling was alarmed.

'I'm not going to mummify you, you eejit.' She covered her sister's scalp in the cling film and then told her to go and knot a towel around it.

Aisling disappeared into the bathroom to do as she was told. She pulled the towel off the rail and twisted it into a turban before glancing in the mirror. Jaysus, if those circles under her eyes got any deeper, she'd look like one of those little red pandas. She'd not been sleeping properly for ages now, not since Quinn proposed. The problem was, each time she was about to nod off, she'd remember something she had to do between now and Valentine's Day and her eyes would fly open and she'd begin panicking. It was a vicious cycle and she didn't know how to calm herself down. She leaned into the mirror and whispered.

Dear Aisling,

I'm getting married in a week and a half and instead of feeling excited about what should be the most amazing day of my life, I'm terrified something's going to go wrong. Please give me some advice as to how I can shake this feeling. Oh, and any tips on how to stop Mrs O'Flaherty trying to tempt me away from my Special K and over to the dark side would be appreciated too.

Yours faithfully,

Me

Mrs Flaherty, their apple-cheeked breakfast cook who worked Monday to Friday was not impressed with the weight loss challenge Bronagh and Aisling had inadvertently undertaken thanks to Moira. She was a woman who did not believe in dieting, although apparently she was partial to the odd bet, but Moira was sworn to secrecy as to who she was backing. She'd been heard to mutter on many an occasion you couldn't trust a person who didn't wipe their plate clean with their bread. Diet was an offensive word and it did not feature in her vocabulary. As such, she was employing sabotage techniques like standing at the bottom of the stairs with a plate of freshly fried, crispy bacon long enough to ensure it didn't go cold by the time it reached the hungry guest who'd ordered it. Long enough though for the tempting aroma to fill the reception area causing the two women to pause in their morning's stair aerobics, mouths watering, resolve weakening. Moira was having none of it though and she'd taken to keeping the can of fancy air freshener Mammy was after recommending on Bronagh's desk. She'd spray it liberally and reception would smell like bacon and Arpège perfume.

Aisling turned side on to peruse her shape in the mirror. So far, she'd avoided temptation and the dance lesson the other night on top of the stairs routine seemed to be yielding results she thought, smoothing her sweater and not seeing any lumps or bumps. She'd never be a waif but aside from the cling film on her head and circles under her eyes she was looking good.

With one last flick over her reflection she went back to the living room where Moira was waiting with a tube of something in her hand. 'A face mask,' she said, waving it. 'It'll work wonders.'

'Is it your clay one?' Aisling said, sitting down.

'No, that's expensive. This one will be grand.'

'Charming, I get the bargain basement beauty treatment. Well, for your information, your whizz bang, pricey one gave me spots anyway.'

'I don't recall you asking me if you could use it,' Moira said.

'It was payback for pinching my Valentino sandals.'

'Fair play.' Moira was feeling magnanimous thanks to a very pleasant few hours whiled away with Tom that afternoon. She squeezed the gloopy green contents of the tube into the palm of her hand and told her sister to look up as she began to slather it all over her face. 'You look a little like Shrek.'

Aisling closed her eyes, not bothered with making a rebuttal. It was nice to be pampered, especially because it meant she had to stop, sit and do nothing for a while. She flexed her feet, her big toe was still tender from where Quinn had trodden on it at their dance lesson. It had brought tears to her eyes, although she didn't know if it was because of that or the fact he'd looked like he had something unpleasant in his pants as he'd minced toward her. She'd finally nailed the razzmatazz as Maria said her opening sequence of steps was called sometime after nine pm when she was nearly dead on her feet and at the same time Antonio had declared he was satisfied with Quinn's tags, taps, kicks and flicks. They were dismissed with an all the best for the wedding by the South American couple who were keen to see the back of their two left footed students and lock up the studio for the night.

'I'm done in,' Quinn had said, and Aisling had told him they'd have to practice every day if they wanted the routine down pat for the wedding. Quinn had muttered something she thought might have been for fecks sake but she couldn't be sure. She'd let it slide given his hang over.

'There we are, all done,' Moira said to her now, holding her green hands up. 'I'll go and wash these. That mask might feel a little tight and tingly but it's nothing to worry about, alright?' Aisling was about to open her mouth and reply but Moira held her green hand up once more, 'Don't speak, let it harden and do its thing.'

It was a chance to reflect on the day, Aisling thought, leaning her head back on the sofa as she mulled things over. The guesthouse had been busy with a group checking out first thing that morning in order to begin their tour around the Irish countryside. Bronagh, thankfully, was running on full throttle once more. The week had gotten off to a slow start for them after their big night out but Bronagh had been particularly pasty-faced on Monday morning. She'd told Moira she could forget it if she had any plans on making her do the stairs and also, she'd better not be thinking about getting married any time soon because she was not able for another hen night. Ita too had been very quiet and Aisling suspected from the length of time it took her to make up Room 3 she might have been having a sly forty winks in there.

She'd let it all waft over her head. It wasn't an everyday occurrence, well at least she didn't think it was. She couldn't be sure when it came to Ita and sure, they'd all had a grand night out together. The mask tightened and her skin began to feel hot beneath it and more than a little tingly. 'Moira,' she called out, feeling it crack around her mouth. 'I'm going to wash this off, it's burning.'

Moira appeared in the doorway. 'It says on the tube you're to leave it on for twenty minutes, it's only been ten.'

'Don't care.' Aisling pushed past her sister to the bathroom and splashed tepid water over her face before getting the nearest flannel and rubbing the stuff off.

'Moira!' she bellowed, looking in the mirror and seeing her face was a blotchy red mass as though she'd gotten the sunburn. 'Get in here now.'

Moira peered around the bathroom door and winced seeing her sister. 'Jaysus, Aisling, you look a fright. You don't want to be going downstairs with your face like that, you'll frighten the guests so you will.'

'Fix it. This is your fault.' Her voice was low and steely and Moira could tell she meant business.

'Listen, you rinse the conditioner out of your hair in case we have to go to the emergency doctors, you don't want to be sitting about in the waiting room with the cling film on your head.'

'Moira!'

'I'll ring Mammy, see what she says.' Moira scarpered. Aisling ran the shower and while she waited for the water to heat, she peered into the mirror. This was not good, her face felt hot and itchy. The last thing she needed was an allergic reaction. She stripped off and got in the shower rinsing off the thick conditioner.

She hoped her skin might have settled down once she got out of the shower but no, if anything the steamy water had made it worse. She got dressed and went in search of Moira.

'Well?'

'Mammy says you're to use the E45 cream.'

Moira held out a tube of their mammy's go-to fix it all cream she'd found tucked away in the first aid kit and Aisling slathered it on. It did feel better.

An hour later when her hair had dried and she was sitting in front of the tele with a greasy layer of E45 all over her face, Moira said, 'At least your hair looks good. If you did a mammy and swished it about you could be on a shampoo commercial. So long as they only filmed you from the back.'

Aisling glared at her.

Her phone beeped a message before she could give her sister a mouthful and she saw it was from Quinn. A frown embedded itself between her eyebrows as she read the message.

'What is it?'

'It's Quinn. He's after finding a house he wants us to go and look at tomorrow.' There was an uneasy feeling in the pit of her stomach at the thought of it.

'You're not moving out of here! I promise I'll stop pinching your shoes and I'm sorry I used the cheap, green shite on your face.' Moira was aghast at the thought of having to do the housework about the place or cooking her own meals.

'You've promised me that before and you always break your word.' Aisling rubbed her temples; her head was hurting. 'But don't worry I'm not going anywhere. The house thing is an investment. He's got a bee in his bonnet that we need to get on the property ladder and rent out whatever we buy as a nest egg. Why he can't wait until after the wedding I don't know but he says here,' she waved her phone, 'it's too good not to go and take a look.' A thought occurred to her. 'What if my face hasn't settled down by tomorrow?'

'Well, it might work in your favour, Ash. The estate agent might tell the people selling about your poor, red, spotty face and they might feel so sorry for you they lower the price.' Her mouth twitched.

'That is so not funny.'

Chapter 25

The house was terraced, red brick, and on the Crumlin Road. Aisling felt a surge of pride as Quinn managed with lots of turning of the steering wheel to manoeuvre his car between two others. The parallel park was not something she'd mastered. Driving was something she'd not mastered all that well for that matter. She could get from A to B so long as the vehicle was an automatic and no complicated parking issues arose but if someone else was happy to drive, then Aisling was happy to let them. If it had been down to her she thought as he pulled the handbrake up, she would have kept driving and they'd have wound up walking miles to their appointment. All thoughts of her masterful-parker fiancé dissipated as she spied the For Sale sign outside a dilapidated house with a sinking heart. She didn't know what she'd been expecting but it was identical to all the other houses on the street. The only thing setting it apart from its neighbours was its air of having been let go.

'It looks neglected,' she said, peering out the windscreen adding an, 'unloved,' for good measure. Quinn had filled her in on the way over; the reason the house was going for a song was because it was an inheritance and the family wanted a quick sale. It explained why it looked unlived in but it didn't make it any more appealing.

'The garden needs a tidy up that's all, and you haven't even seen inside yet, Ash.' He took the keys from the ignition and turned in his seat to look at her. He looked away quickly for fear she'd think he was staring at the lumps that had appeared on her face since the last time he'd seen her. Hives she'd said, due to a dodgy facial Moira had given her. He thought it as likely it was a reaction to all the stress she was heaping upon herself with the wedding. There was no point saying anything though.

Aisling could feel the heels of her shoes digging into the mat on the floor of the passenger seat and her hands were clasped tightly, resting on her black pencil skirt. She'd dressed up for the occasion in the hope of moving the focus from her face. The fact she'd power dressed though had done nothing to change her mind where this house buying business was concerned and she'd be quite happy if Quinn were to manoeuvre his way back out of the parking space. She'd give the suited-up man with the slicked back hair who was tapping his foot beside the gate, a cheery wave goodbye as they sailed past him. In fact, what she'd like, more than anything, was for them to go and get a cup of coffee and talk like they hadn't talked in ages. She wanted reassurance he was excited about their nuptials because she felt like he'd switched off.

'And he's definitely got the look of a fecky brown noser,' she muttered, turning her attention back to the waiting agent.

'What was that?' Quinn asked, opening his door.

'Nothing.'

'Come on then and keep an open mind. Remember it needs to be low maintenance and functional, that's all. It's not your dream home, it's a potential rental property.'

'Yes, yes, I will.' She was already picturing patches of damp, and mouse poo, and all manner of unsavoury things given the neglected air of the garden.

Quinn glanced back at her dubiously. 'If we can get it for the right price, the rent should cover the loan and outgoings. It comes down to the maths not emotions.'

'I know that.' Aisling was huffy. It seemed to her he'd already made his mind up about buying the place and he sounded a little condescending. She wasn't an airhead. All she wanted was her wedding to be her perfect day without major life distractions like house buying getting in the way. She didn't want them starting their married life by being saddled with a money-pit of a house they had no plans of living in either. Nevertheless, she got out of the car and waited for Quinn to lock it before walking the short distance to the estate agent, who stepped forward with his hand outstretched to greet them. He was all smiles, although Aisling fancied his full wattage beam had faltered as she got closer.

The E45 cream had helped soothe the itching but the spots were still visible and she'd made Moira run down to Boots as soon as it opened to buy a packet of antihistamines out of her own pocket. She'd taken one as soon as her sister returned and hoped the hives would soon begin to fade. For now, though, at least her hair was shining gloriously and she lurked alongside Quinn observing the vigorous handshaking and much fecky brown nosing on the agent's part. His name he revealed before opening the gate, its rusty hinge squeaking in protest, was Niall. Holding it open he ushered them in and Aisling trailed behind Quinn, her heel finding its way into a crack in the pavers which nearly sent her arse about face.

'Watch your step,' Niall said pointlessly. 'The path and front garden needs a little TLC but it's all easily fixed and the house has good bones.'

With a glance to either side she could see the poky front garden was in desperate need of a tidy up. What had once grown there, maybe even flourished, had now withered and needed to be cut back. She couldn't stop her nose curling even though she knew it made her look a spoiled brat. She also wished Quinn didn't have such a spring in his step. He looked like a child about to enter a sweet shop and his new best friend Niall's eyes were gleaming no doubt at the thought of the hefty commission soon to be coming his way if he played this the right way. He produced a bunch of keys and stepping past them unlocked the front door opening it wide.

'Come in, come in,' he welcomed with a sweep of his hand.

Aisling took a deep breath and stepped over the threshold, scanning the hallway she found herself in with a critical eye. It was narrow and dark with a threadbare red carpet adding to the gloom. You'd struggle to swing a cat in it she thought as Niall announced he'd let them have a look around on their own. It was all self-explanatory he said and when they were finished, they'd find him in the kitchen. She watched him stride down the hall, counting his steps. Four strides and he was there. It was hardly a house you'd get lost in.

Quinn was opening a cupboard in the hallway and hearing him make noises about how it was good to have extra storage space, she left him to inspect it, poking her head around the front room. Through the yellowing net curtains, she could see the outline of the garden they'd walked past and in the same red carpet as she'd seen in the hall, she could see the indents of where the furniture had been placed. The wallpaper was peeling in places and the room smelt musty. A layer of dust was visible over the fireplace mantle.

She didn't want to look around any further because she already knew the kitchen where Niall was waiting was at the end of the hall. It would have an oven with decades of food etched around the element rings. A washing line that spun around would be visible from the back window and the back garden would be bleaker than the front entrance. Upstairs there would be a bathroom with pipes that would gurgle and moan when the hot water tap was turned and the bedrooms would be boxy. It was exactly what she'd expected. Quinn had joined her in the room and must have sensed she was less than impressed as he nudged her and said, 'Use your imagination, Ash, a lick of paint, new curtains and carpet, some elbow grease and sure, it will be grand.'

They made their way to the back of the house to check out the kitchen before heading upstairs. Niall was there as he'd said he'd be. He was leaning against the sink but spying his potential purchasers sprang into action, gesturing to the cupboards and pantry. Quinn was all ears as the agent launched into a spiel. 'Retro's all the rage, although of course, for the discerning investor there's plenty of scope for improvement.' He leaned toward them conspiratorially. 'Quinn, Aisling, between me and you, this area's rapidly becoming sought after, and properties are tightly held. It's a good time to buy.'

Quinn nodded and opened a drawer. He gave it an extra tug as it got stuck halfway nearly pulling the whole thing out. Aisling eyed the oven, noticing the splashes of grease on the wall behind it. She fancied she could smell bacon fat and not in a tempting Mrs Flaherty way either. She pondered over opening the back door to get some fresh air but decided against it. The sooner they completed their tour of the house the sooner she'd be out of here. Instead she contented herself with looking out the window to where a spindly tree waved its boughs in the wind and a washing line spun round in a maniacal pirouette. The fence surrounding the nondescript garden was buckled in places. Quinn nudged her. 'Are you ready to take a look upstairs.'

She nodded and followed him from the room, refusing to look at Niall for fear of setting him off on more sales patter. Quinn skipped up the stairs and she bunny-hopped up them after him, her skirt making it impossible to do anything else, wondering if the musty smell permeating downstairs would be worse up there. Quinn wandered in and out of the first two bedrooms while she gave them a cursory glance over. The bathroom made her shudder but if she were honest, she could see all it needed was a good scrub. The shower head was over the bath and the plastic curtain had a mouldy edge to it. It was a set-up that brought to mind the verruca she'd gotten one year at the public baths. She couldn't muster up enthusiasm to match Quinn's as he turned the handle on the shower and announced the pressure was good. She let him lead her through to the smallest of the three bedrooms not listening to his prattle that it was big enough for a small double. He was already wording the advert to rent the house in his head, she realised, seeing his face was lit up with an excitement she hadn't once seen in the march toward their wedding.

'Ash,' he said, opening the wardrobe door and poking his head inside it.

'Yes.' He was taking leaving no door unopened to a new level. A wardrobe was a wardrobe for fecks sake and she played out a scenario where she pushed him inside it and shut the door.

He popped back out and the sight of his eager face sent guilt pinpricking through her. He only wanted the best for them. It wasn't very nice of her to be plotting to shove him inside a cupboard. He couldn't read her mind though and carried on excitedly, 'I think we should go for it. Subject to a building inspection obviously but I can't see how we can go wrong.'

She could see he wanted her to agree with him. To share in his enthusiasm but she couldn't. What he was saying about financial security and investments for the future all made sense but she had a bad feeling. 'I'm not trying to burst your bubble, Quinn, but I have a lot on my plate at the moment with the wedding.' She shook her head, 'I'm struggling to find room to think about anything else.'

'I know that, Ash. But if we don't act now, we'll miss out. Who knows when a buy like this will come up again?'

Quinn didn't often dig his heels in. He was the sort of fella who went with the flow but he wanted this property, she could see it in the determined set of his jaw. She wanted to react the way he wanted her to, she did. He deserved it. Sure, look at the way he'd agreed to their honeymoon at the Ice Hotel. Marriage was about compromise and this was her moment to capitulate and agree, yes this would indeed be a good investment for them. He placed his hands on either side of the tops of her arms his blue eyes boring into hers, willing her to agree.

'It doesn't have to be hard, Ash. We can arrange to take possession after our honeymoon. It'll be one visit to the bank, there'll be a few papers to be signed with a solicitor, that's all. I'll arrange the building inspection but I think we should move on this. It's a smart move. We'll regret it if we procrastinate.' She barely heard him as he told her the figure he'd like to offer. She trusted him to have worked it all out but still the words he wanted to hear wouldn't come. She managed another nod, wanting to make him happy. There was a part of her that loved the way he was thinking ahead for them and for, hopefully, one day in the not too distant future, their children. He pulled her to him and she enjoyed the feeling of security being in his arms always gave her. 'Do I take that as a yes, let's go for it?'

'Yes.'

Her reward was a kiss and she returned it, glad he was pleased and wishing she could get rid of the sense of unease that had assailed her since she received his text the night before. He held her hand tightly as they headed back down the stairs to find Niall. He looked up from his phone as they appeared in the kitchen once more.

'Well, what did you think?'

'We can definitely see the potential,' Quinn countered.

Niall sensed he had them on the hook and in case they hadn't heard him the first time he repeated his earlier sentiment of this being a sought-after area and how he had another couple interested in viewing the property. The sense of urgency he was instilling in them made Aisling feel panicked, which was what he intended, but her head had started to hurt again, too. She was supposed to be meeting Leila in an hour and now she'd agreed to go ahead and do this, she wanted Quinn to cut to the chase and make an offer so they could find out whether or not it would be accepted and she could put some distance between herself and Niall.

Quinn squeezed her hand. 'We'd like to make an offer,' he said, before repeating the figure he'd told her he thought they should put on the table. Niall looked pleased but gave no clue as to whether they stood a chance going in with the figure, he'd just been given. He pulled his phone from his jacket pocket and tapped out a phone number his face a blank canvas as he waited for it to be answered. Despite her misgivings, now they'd come this far, Aisling wanted it all to pan out. She found herself holding her breath as Niall began to speak and Quinn's grip on her hand became vicelike. The agent was Mr Cool as he relayed their price. His end of the conversation gave nothing away and it wasn't until he'd hung up, he flashed his mega smile and said, 'If you're prepared to stretch to another two thousand then you've got yourselves a deal.'

Quinn glanced to Aisling and she mouthed go for it. What difference, given the vast sums involved with buying a house, would two thousand punt make?

There were a few hurdles to jump before they got to the finish line though. The other couple might come in with a better offer, the building inspection might throw up unseen issues, or Mr Cleary might turn down their application for a mortgage. Niall however was full of bonhomie and as they went left and he turned to the right outside the front gate. Aisling was tempted to look back over her shoulder to see if he was fist bumping the air or doing an excitable shin to shin side kick like in the old movies. She didn't though, focussing instead on steadying her breathing and wishing Rosi was there with her. She had tricks up her sleeve that would help make you feel calmer and she could have done with her sister intoning, 'in, and out' in that irritating hypnotic voice she used. It was only when she was settled in the passenger seat of Quinn's car once more, she felt able to catch her breath. Quinn was on a high and he talked all the way to Blackrock slapping the steering wheel from time to time, the adrenalin coursing through his bloodstream. She barely heard him as he yapped on about whether they should renovate the kitchen which might generate a better rental or leave it as it was until they'd paid a chunk off the house.

His grin however was infectious as he pulled up outside the charming whitewashed building from which Leila ran Love Leila Bridal Services. Her mouth twitched and stretched into a broad smile. She was pleased he was pleased and she was sure she'd come around to the idea. It did make sense. 'Right then.' Quinn slapped the steering wheel once more. 'I'll phone Michael and get the wheels in motion.'

'Who?' she frowned, her mind drawing a blank at the name.

'You know *Michael.*'

She looked at him blankly and he sighed. 'Ash, you're so old school. Mr Cleary from the AIB.'

'Oh, yeah of course. Sorry.' She'd never get her head around calling a bank manager by his first name.

'He'll probably want to check through our accounts to see everything is in order before approving the loan but he seemed fairly confident it wouldn't be a problem the other day.'

And there it was, the reason Aisling felt sick about this property. It was nothing to do with the weeds sprouting through the cracked pavers, or the ancient oven and old carpets. It was the thought of that old bloodhound, Mr Cleary, poring over her bank statements and realising not only did she not have an outstanding savings record, but she had these last couple of weeks been spending up large. Astronomically so. Bank account draining so. She was frightened as to what Quinn would have to say when he found out exactly what this wedding of theirs was costing because her gut instinct told her, he would not be happy.

She tried to brush aside the sudden panic not wanting him to pick up on anything being amiss. His lips felt papery as they grazed her flushed skin and telling him she'd speak to him later, she turned the handle and clambered out of the car. It was a relief to put some distance between them.

Chapter 26

The aroma of freshly brewed coffee assailed Aisling's nostrils as she pushed the door open and stepped into the warmth of Leila's familiar work space. There was comfort to be found, knowing that, in the small kitchenette out the back, there would be a plate with the fresh French pastries her friend picked up for her clients to enjoy on her way into work each morning. She loved the calming and neutral colours Leila had chosen to decorate the office with. They hadn't been chosen randomly she'd confided to Aisling. The pale pastels adorning the walls and soft furnishings were designed to counteract the nervous tension of her brides. The idea was that Leila's was a haven where the pressure of trying to keep both sides of the family, along with the bridal party, happy during the lead up to your wedding dissolved once you stepped over the threshold.

Leila's goal was for her brides to feel confident she had their dream day under control. She wanted them to sink down in the sofa and let her fuss around making them coffee. Then, she wanted to see their shoulders visibly unknot as they forgot their diets and tucked into a well-deserved buttery croissant while she brought them up to date with the planning of their big day. The feminine pink walls were adorned with black and white prints of famous brides through the decades. Aisling's favourite, and the one her gaze always settled upon, was Audrey Hepburn. Inexplicably, this was because she always felt like she was gazing upon a fairy when she looked at the elegant, time-less beauty.

Now, as she stood in the entrance swivelling in her heels on the mat in case there'd been anything untoward on those threadbare carpets at the Crumlin Road property, she un-clenched her jaw. It would take more than the sanctuary of Leila's to relieve her headache though, it was a constant, dull pressure above her right eye. A little like a hangover which wasn't very fair because she hadn't been drinking the night before and did not deserve this punishment. Leila glanced up from her worktable, straightening the papers she'd been poring over and placing them back in a folder. She looked especially pretty today with her hair twisted back in a loose plait which softened the look of her fitted pant suit. For Leila's part, she gave her friend a cursory once over. 'You mean business, Ash,' she said, taking in the jacket and skirt ensemble. She hesitated as she registered the lumpy blotches decorating her friend's face. 'What happened?'

For the briefest of moments, Aisling wondered if her un-ease about the wedding was written all over her face. Leila knew her inside and out after all, but then she remembered the hives and even though she knew it wouldn't help matters her hand touched her cheek rubbing at the itching patches self-consciously. 'Do you mean these?'

Leila nodded. 'Don't rub it. You'll only make it worse.' She was hoping it wasn't some sort of facial shingles brought on by stress. If it was, then Aisling had brought it on herself. It was exasperating insomuch as she'd offered her services as a gift to make sure her best friend relaxed and enjoyed every minute of the lead up to her big day. Despite her best efforts to convince her it was all coming together nicely, Aisling seemed intent on winding herself up into a permanent state of anxiety. She'd even seen her biting her nails the other day, a habit she'd grown out of in her early teens.

'In one word, Moira. That's what happened.'

'What did she do?' Leila was bewildered.

'She gave me a facial last night, that's what, and she used this cheap, green shite that resulted in an allergic reaction.'

Leila clamped her lips together to try to stop the giggle threatening to burst forth as she imagined the scenario post-facial in the family apartment at O'Mara's last night. She wouldn't have liked to be Moira but it would have been funny to be a fly on the wall.

'You better not laugh,' Aisling warned, wagging a finger at her. 'Because I don't feel like laughing, I feel like crying.'

'Oh, Ash, what's wrong? And I wasn't going to laugh,' Leila lied, forcing herself to swallow the giddy bubbles of mirth. 'Honestly, your face. It's not that bad. I hardly even noticed it.'

Aisling glared at her. 'When someone says 'honestly',' she made inverted fingers, 'they're always lying.'

'Okay, sorry, but they'll go right?' Have you got something for them?'

Aisling nodded. 'Mammy put us onto the E45 cream which helped a little and I made Moira go to Boots first thing too. She hadn't even done her hair and she said it was mortifying which served her right because this,' she jabbed in the direction of her face, 'is mortifying.'

Leila concentrated on keeping her face in a duly concerned expression.

'They should be gone by tomorrow,' Aisling continued. 'And if they're not then she will be demoted from her position as bridesmaid to toilet attendant duties at the reception.'

At the picture invoked of Moira handing out wads of toilet paper in exchange for penny donations, Leila did laugh.

Aisling wasn't trying to be funny though. 'It's not my face that's bothering me. Well, it is obviously, because no one wants to walk around with itchy, red lumps by choice but it's not why I feel sick.'

Here we go, Leila thought, donning her professional hat. She was well versed with comforting her brides to be, she prided herself on her ability to do so, but on a scale of one to ten Aisling was coming in at a nine-and-a-half on the Bridezilla scale. 'You poor thing, come on, sit yourself down on the sofa and I'll get you a cup of coffee.' She hesitated, normally she'd offer a pastry but Aisling was supposed to be dieting.

Aisling solved her conundrum, 'And can I have a pastry. One of the ones with the drizzle of white icing and chocolate filling? Please.'

'Of course, you can.'

Aisling flopped down on the sofa and pulled the cushion out from behind her back hugging it to her stomach. Leila who'd been about to head to the kitchenette paused, her mouth dropping open.

'Why are you looking at me like I suddenly sprouted a second head?'

'Ash, oh my God, you're not pregnant, are you?' Leila whispered the word pregnant as though disapproving eyes were everywhere, her own were like blue gobstoppers.

'What?' Aisling glanced down at her midriff and realising she was holding the cushion over it. She tossed it down the opposite end of the two-seater before smoothing out her sweater. Not quite flat as a pancake but hardly six months gone. 'No, wash your mouth out.'

'Jaysus! You had me worried there. It was with you saying you felt sick and then asking for a pastry and the bulge of the cushion.' Leila fanned her face with her hand at the shock of it all as her voice trailed off. She had enough sense not to add that given Aisling had also been behaving like a hormonal wreck these last weeks she could hardly be blamed for jumping to conclusions. Instead, she said, 'Sorry, Ash. I'll go make that coffee and then you can tell me all about it. How does that sound?'

Aisling leaned her back against the plush fabric, placated. 'Grand. Oh, and Leila don't tell anyone about the pastry, okay? There's money involved.'

'I won't.' She tapped the side of her nose. 'It's our secret.'

Leila disappeared out the back and Aisling consciously tried to relax. She flexed her fingers and rolled her head around in slow circles. Everything would be alright. It would all be fine. She was paranoid that was all, once burned and all that. Sure, in just over a week she'd be Mrs Aisling O'Mara-Moran and the stress of the build-up would be behind her. All she'd be left with were stunning photographs and her memories. It'd be like what she'd heard about giving birth, you forgot all about the icky bits afterward. By the time Leila returned to place a pretty china mug with a curl of steam rising from it in front of her, along with a plate on which the promised pastry sat, she was feeling better. She nibbled on the sweet treat and equilibrium was restored as the sugar hit her bloodstream. Leila returned with her own coffee and once Aisling saw she was settled down the other end of the sofa, she began to talk.

Chapter 27

'Did I tell you Quinn has been making noises about us buying a house as an investment?' Aisling dabbed up the pastry flakes on her plate as she waited for her friend to reply.

'No, you didn't.'

'His idea is that we'll pick up a doer upper, that doesn't need too much doing up and rent it out. We'll pay it off that way.'

'Not a silly idea,' Leila said, sipping her drink and looking over the rim at Aisling.

'It's not, I agree, and I love the way he's thinking about our future but you have to admit his timing is shite.'

'What do you mean?'

'I mean the wedding obviously. It's all I can think about and there's no room for big decisions like enormous loans and the like. It's not fair of him to add all this pressure to the mix now.'

'You shouldn't be feeling pressured. I have everything in hand. It's my job and I'm good at it.' She was wasting her breath, Leila thought as Aisling ploughed on.

'Then today he insisted we go and see a house on the Crumlin Road. He said it looked like a good buy and got himself all excited, more excited than I've seen him in weeks. I don't think he even got that worked up when I bought a suspender belt and stockings that time. Sod of a thing they were, kept pinging off.' She shook her head at the memory. 'Anyway, he was like a child exploring Disneyland and, Leila, his face has not once been as animated over our wedding as it was when he was looking around that run-down old terrace today. Not once.' It was true, Aisling thought, reliving the memories of his face closing up every time she mentioned something to do with the wedding.

'I wouldn't be reading anything into that, Aisling. You know how it goes, "Men are from Mars, women are from Venus.". Well, it's true. I have yet to see a groom who is wrapped up in the details of his wedding to the same degree as his bride. They don't understand the importance of the small details.' She shrugged. 'All they want is their stag night to be unforgettable, then to front up on the day and have it all to run smoothly. That's it. They are simple creatures.'

Aisling was almost mollified but instinct told her it was more than a lack of interest it was almost as if he wanted to bury his head in the sand over the whole thing.

'He's doing his part isn't he? Organising his and his brothers' suits and the wedding rings.'

It was Aisling's turn to shrug. 'I don't know. Every time I broach the subject, he changes it. Look what he did today. Why did we need to buy a house right now?'

Leila nearly slopped her coffee. 'You bought it?'

'We made an offer on it and it was accepted.'

'Congratulations! That's fantastic, Ash. What's it like?'

'A standard terrace house that has been let go.'

Leila frowned. She could see she wasn't going to get much more from her friend. 'Well, I think it's a fantastic start to your married life.'

'We're not married yet.'

'You will be in just over a week.'

'If Quinn doesn't call the whole thing off.'

Leila had had enough. 'For feck's sake, Aisling!' She banged her cup down on the table startling her friend who was slumping further down the couch the more she wallowed. 'Snap out of it. This has got to stop. You are a woman on the edge of a nervous breakdown.'

Aisling made to protest and defend her corner, but she'd pushed Leila too far.

'It's ridiculous. You're behaving like a complete and utter eejit over this wedding.'

Hot tears burned in Aisling's green eyes and the hives heated up. This wasn't Leila's job. Leila's job as her best friend was to listen and agree with her while simultaneously making murmuring noises of support. Moira and Mammy were the only ones in their pecking order allowed to speak to her this way.

'Why won't you accept Quinn loves you?'

Aisling sniffed and Leila passed her the tissues kept on the table for those emotional moments. Aisling pulled one from the box and dabbed her eyes.

'In ten days, Aisling, you two are going to be married but your insecurity is spoiling what should be a happy time for you both!'

Aisling blew her nose. Leila was right. It was her ruining everything but now she had good reason to be insecure. 'Leila,' she managed to get a word in before she could head off on another tangent. 'You don't understand.'

'Help me understand then because I thought you'd finally got it through that head of yours, things not working out once before doesn't mean history will repeat itself.' Leila looked at her expectantly.

Aisling took a shuddering breath and her voice wavered a little as she began to speak. 'There's been this fear from the moment I accepted Quinn's proposal something would go wrong before we could head down the aisle.' Aisling twisted the edge of her sweater. 'And now it has.' A sob caught at the back of her throat.

Leila passed her the tissue box once more. 'Here, take one.'

She helped herself giving her nose another quick blow. 'We have to have our loan to buy the house approved by Mr Cleary at the bank. He was working out our borrowings based on the deposit we agreed to come up with for whatever we decided to buy.'

Leila nodded. 'That's standard.'

'Yes, but when Quinn first broached this with me not long after Christmas we sat down together and worked out a figure based on our joint savings. That's what he worked our offer on the Crumlin Road property around. The thing is, I've been spending since then Leila. I've been spending a lot. I don't even know how much because I haven't been keeping tabs but I do know I don't have anywhere near what I had in my account before we started putting this wedding together. I can't see how we're going to be able to go ahead with the purchase.'

Leila tilted her head to one side. She was beginning to understand what had Aisling so worked up. She had been splashing the cash what with horse-drawn pumpkin carriages, pricey photographers, a Swarovski crystal embossed dress, not to mention her insistence on splurging on all the bridesmaids' dresses and they'd been almost as eyewatering in price as the wedding gown. She'd tried to broach how much it was all costing with Aisling a couple of times but she'd been so caught up in the dream of her day she hadn't wanted any reality checks. A memory struck her. 'Your dress, Ash, that's my fault. I broke my golden rule. I showed you it before telling you what it cost. It was just so—'

Aisling held her hand up, 'Gorgeous? I know, and you hardly had to twist my arm.' And now I've gone and paid the deposit on the honeymoon too.' She winced at the memory of the smiling travel agent handing over her credit card receipt. She'd even passed her the bowl of complimentary mints. A sure sign she'd spent up large. But again, Quinn had never asked her anything more about the honeymoon. Sure, he'd made a few vague inquiries about what it cost but he'd been content to leave the arrangements up to her.

'You've kept him up to date with everything, haven't you? I mean you guys are a dream team.' Leila was struggling with the idea Aisling had gone ahead and booked what equated to the best of everything without once checking in with her future husband.

Aisling gave a small shake of her head and felt a current of anger at her fiancé's lacklustre approach to their wedding. If he'd been willing to share in it all, to contribute to the planning then she wouldn't have got herself in such a mess. The more he'd tuned out over it all, the more she'd amped things up in the bling stakes. It was very tempting to pass the blame onto Quinn. She'd like to take her anger and run with it because it was better than the sensation of impending doom she was currently saddled with. It hadn't been him wielding the credit card like he was a Saudi prince though. Oh no, the blame for that sat squarely on her shoulders and she was not a member of the Saudi royal family, she was Aisling O'Mara of O'Mara's Guesthouse on the Green.

'No, I haven't told him. He has no idea what it's all costing and I'm petrified when he finds out he's going to call the wedding off.

Chapter 28

Aisling got back to the guesthouse with Leila's advice she needed to sit down and talk things through with Quinn before they went to see their bank manager ringing in her ears. It would be far better for him to find out exactly how much this wedding had depleted their finances first-hand than through some know-it-all with a name badge at the AIB she'd warned. Aisling knew she was right. She had to come clean and she resolved to go and see Quinn as soon as she'd checked in at O'Mara's and gotten changed. The snug waistband of her skirt was a reminder of her pastry misdemeanour and besides, the conversation she was about to have with Quinn warranted comfortable trousers. There was a modicum of relief in a decision having been made as to what she needed to do but still and all, it was a confession she wasn't looking forward to having to make.

Bronagh was sliding her arms into the sleeves of her coat. Nina was yet to arrive, Aisling realised, scanning the reception area, and Bronagh had a pinched look about her as though she'd eaten an olive thinking it was a grape. She hoped everything was alright. 'Have you an appointment you've got to get to?' she inquired, fishing for information.

'Jaysus wept, Aisling, you look like you've been ravished by a mosquito. What happened to your face?'

Aisling sighed and repeated the sorry tale of cheap skincare products and her selfish mare of a sister. Bronagh listened with half an ear, commenting if Moira passed herself as an expert in the beauty stakes and got results like the ones currently decorating Aisling's face, could she be trusted when it came to her foray into personal training? Aisling got the impression she was desperate for a legitimate excuse to get out of tomorrow morning's stair climbing. She picked her bag up but before she could leave, Aisling repeated her question. 'Do you have somewhere important you need to be?' It was asked without guile and a hint of concern.

'No, I'm in need of fresh air that's all, Aisling.' Bronagh flicked her eyes about the place and satisfied the coast was clear muttered, 'I've had it up to here today.' She saluted her forehead several times to prove her point before picking up a piece of paper and thrusting it in Aisling's direction. 'It's enough to turn a woman to drink so it is.' The crumbs on the desk in front of her suggested she hadn't turned to alcohol but had found comfort in her custard cream biscuits instead. Good, Aisling thought, quietly pleased she wasn't the only one who'd had an indiscretion this afternoon. She scanned the piece of paper, understanding dawning as to why their receptionist wasn't her usual sunny self. Her own fingers twitched with the urge to reach for one of the custard cream filled biscuits.

The Australian couple who were staying in Room 6 had complained the hot water pressure wasn't great and they'd found a hair belonging to neither of them in the bath. Not only that but the pillows were lumpy and the bed was too hard and hadn't been vacuumed under. She sighed all the way down to the tips of her patent leather, Dior stilettos. Bloody Ita! She'd be having words about her standard of cleaning. It wouldn't be the first time she'd had to rake her over the coals for her slapdash efforts and she knew from past experience their director of housekeeping was a sulker. They'd all be in for days of hoover banging on the skirtings as a result. Still, she needed to be told. As for the hot water pressure, there was nothing wrong with it. Did they want a water blaster to take the fecking skin off them? None of their other guests had ever moaned about lumpy pillows or hard beds either.

Aisling knew the couple's type. They were people for whom there would always be too much salt in the stew or not enough pepper on their steak. The kind who felt short-changed by life in general. Born complainers, and born complainers had to be handled with kid gloves to ensure they didn't make a loud noise in front of their other, perfectly happy guests. There was a saying when it came to offering a service such as their guesthouse, 'the customer was always right.' As such, it was time to don her fecky brown noser hat; Quinn would have to wait.

The door opened as Aisling screwed up the paper and tossed it in the bin and Nina, her face peeping out from the furry hood of her parker, called out an apology for being late. Bronagh, huffing, made her escape out the door and Aisling seeing Nina's face fall, explained. 'You're only a few minutes late, it's not you. Don't worry about Bronagh, she's had a day of it with the couple in Room 6. Full of moans about the place so they are.'

Nina's worried face softened. She hated upsetting people. She was a pleaser and as such she would not ask Aisling why her face was covered in red lumps. She went to hang her coat up in the small kitchen area as Aisling sat down in the seat still warm from Bronagh and placed a call to Room 6 to see if they'd like to have a chat, in the guests' lounge, about how she could improve their stay at a time that suited them.

The sniffy accented twang of Mrs Trope agreed to come down and meet with her in fifteen minutes. Aisling hung up the phone and vacated the seat for Nina before scanning their bookings and seeing, as she'd hoped, Room 8 with its California king was free for the next few nights. An upgrade would hopefully appease them.

AN HOUR LATER, HAVING politely listened to a lengthy rehashing of Mr and Mrs Trope's earlier complaints, Aisling stood in her stocking feet in her bedroom, the skirt with its merciless waistband in a heap next to her feet. She was opening and closing drawers in search of her favourite pyjama bottoms. The headache that had been lurking all day had worsened to an almost migraine-like status and she needed to lie prone on the couch and let the paracetamol she'd popped work their magic. She also needed to indulge in a few snowballs which always had the exact opposite effect on her headaches, chocolate was supposed to have. Her favourite coconutty, chocolicious treat and an hour spent staring gormlessly at the television should sort her out. Then, she'd go to Quinn's.

Moira blessedly was out so the apartment was silent and she could put whatever tripe she fancied on the box and vegetate. Bliss. She deserved it after the grovelling she'd had to do where the Tropes were concerned. It had gone against the grain to place such an ungrateful pair of heathens in a larger suite, especially as she'd gotten a vibe from them upgrades were something they were well-practised at getting. She had them marked down as the kind of couple who creates a scene by saying there was a cockroach in their dinner in order to get out of paying the bill. In the long run though, it was easier to move and appease them than have the duo upset the equilibrium amongst their other guests. They were checking out the day after tomorrow. It was a small price to pay.

She'd positioned herself so she was spread the length of the sofa like an aging film star except instead of grapes she had a bowl of the snowballs within hands reach. She'd hidden them for emergency situations like this, behind the baked beans in the cupboard where Moira would not find them (she hated baked beans). A ridiculous game show was flickering on the screen in front of her with a paunchy, balding man who fancied himself a comedian hosting it. It was his blonde sidekick in the scanty evening wear who had her mesmerised though. Her facial expressions should see her in line for an Oscar. One minute she was feigning excitement akin to an orgasmic experience when a contestant won an iron and ironing board, the next great sorrow on a par with having found herself orphaned when they lost out on the toaster. The pinging of her phone distracted her. It lay abandoned on the kitchen worktop and she twisted her head to see if she could telepathically get it to float over to where she lay. She squinted her eyes and focussed but it didn't budge and she wondered whether she was strong enough to ignore it. All she wanted was another forty-five minutes or so to lie here and wallow in snowballs and gameshows.

She'd almost convinced herself it had never made a sound when a few minutes later it announced the arrival of another message. One could be ignored but not two, and with a sigh she swung her legs off the sofa and sat up. Her headache had eased which was a bonus and at least she knew it wouldn't be Mammy messaging her. She never bothered with their mobile phones which meant it might actually be something important. 'So long as it wasn't from Quinn,' she muttered, padding over to retrieve the black Nokia. She didn't bother to look at the first message knowing it would be much the same as the second one she'd just read. She wished she had ignored it because from the terse few lines telling her they needed to talk with not one single x or o at the end, Aisling knew Quinn had beaten her to it. He'd already been in touch with Mr Cleary.

Chapter 29

A isling hadn't bothered to run a comb through her hair or put her lipstick on, having decided it was best she go and swallow whatever medicine Quinn was going to dish out. She only went so far as to swap her pyjama bottoms for jeans. She half-heartedly hoped the sight of her wan, spotty face might soften his heart a little.

Alasdair hadn't quite been his usual effusive self, greeting her as she pushed the door of the bistro open and stepped inside. She was unsure if it was out of politeness to avoid mentioning her spots or because he knew what a spendthrift she'd been. Common sense told her it was far more likely it was her guilty conscience playing paranoid tricks on her. She hadn't imagined Quinn's steely expression as he asked her to give him a few minutes before he joined her out on the floor, though. A chill akin to icy fingers had traipsed up and down her spine at his unflinching blue eyes as he paused with the pan of boiling potatoes, he'd been carrying over to the sink to drain. They were eyes that usually twinkled with unspent mirth but tonight they were stormy. His mouth too had been set like a heart monitor flatlining. She'd also caught Paula and Tony glancing at each other before putting their heads down and getting on with the business of making sure the restaurant ticked over. The boss and his fiancée might be at odds but for them it was business as usual.

Aisling had done as he'd suggested, grateful to see Tom wasn't rostered on, as she'd gone in search of a quiet table. She tucked herself into the darkened corner far enough away from the other diners to ensure they weren't privy to her and Quinn's private goings on. From where she'd positioned herself, she could see the fire with its flames, forked tongues of orange and yellow. A shadowy glow danced up the walls, illuminating the framed photographs of guests enjoying boisterous nights in the bistro. She watched a man excuse himself from the pretty woman he was dining with, and saw him dip his head to avoid the low hung ceiling beams as he made his way to the bathroom. There was no band playing tonight given it was early in the week so she and Quinn would, at least, be able to hear themselves speak. She almost wished Shay and his band were on the empty stage banging out a bit of Van Morrison so she didn't have to sit through the talking-to, she knew was coming her way.

Her hands pleated the table napkin for want of something to do with them and she turned her gaze to the salt and pepper shakers in an effort to avoid making eye contact with Paula who was clearing a nearby table. Her corneas were beginning to burn from not blinking when Quinn's voice startled her.

He loomed over the table making her feel small and inconsequential. It wasn't like him to take such a bullying stance. 'I don't understand you, Aisling.' It was said loudly enough to turn the heads of the couple at the closest table. Aisling glared at them, daring them to say anything. They went back to their meals.

'Sit down and lower your voice, Quinn,' she ordered, forgetting she'd planned on being contrite and sufficiently grovelling so he could say his piece and be done with it.

He pulled a chair out and sat down heavily across from her before pulling a folded wad of papers from his pockets which he spread on the table in front of her. The light was dim but not dim enough she couldn't see she was looking at a printout from their joint account.

'When we opened this account, we had this much to put into it.' He jabbed at a figure she couldn't quite make out at the top of the row of numbers. Nevertheless, she nodded before looking away not able to sustain eye contact with him when he was clearly furious. 'The problem is, Aisling, this much has gone out since we opened the account. He shuffled the papers and pointed to another piece of paper. 'And this is now our balance.'

He paused and she wasn't sure what he expected her to do, gasp suitably aghast at her expenditure maybe? When she remained silent, he carried on. 'The balance in our account is nothing like it was when we applied for our loan at the AIB because in the space of a few weeks you've spent it on – hmm, let me see,'

Aisling wanted to put her hands over her ears as he began to reel off a list of expenses that had, at the time, seemed so necessary in the planning of their wedding day but now, listening to the sums involved, came across as ludicrous luxuries nobody in their right mind needed. She wondered if pleading temporary insanity might help her case.

At last his voice trailed off and she looked up. 'I'm sorry,' she squeaked, hoping to see the anger leach from his face.

'Sorry isn't good enough, Aisling. We're going to lose out on the Crumlin Road property because you had to have flowers that cost enough to feed a small nation and a honeymoon in a fecking igloo.'

She opened her mouth to protest but no sound came out and Quinn jumped in once more. 'We don't have enough for the deposit anymore.' The anger had gone out of his voice, replaced by a weariness that to Aisling's mind was far more worrying.

'I'm sorry,' she repeated, not knowing what else to say.

'What's it all for?'

'I don't understand?'

'A horse drawn carriage. I mean for fecks sake, Aisling.'

She tried to summon up the words to explain all the extravagance but couldn't because she didn't understand it herself.

'I tried to involve you.' The words sounded feeble to her own ears and trying to pass the buck wasn't going to make their situation any better.

'Not hard enough obviously.'

Anger rankled. 'Hang on a minute, Quinn. That's not fair. *I did try* but every time I brought the topic up you tuned out so, I went ahead and did what I thought was best. You've not shown any interest in our wedding from the get-go.'

'Oh, so you behaving like you're Victoria fecking Beckham is all my fault, is it?'

'I didn't say that but maybe if you'd sat down with me once or twice and looked at some of my suggestions, we might have found some middle ground.'

Quinn made an unattractive snorting noise. 'There's been no middle ground where this wedding's concerned, not from the moment you accepted my proposal. You've been like a woman possessed.' He hesitated as though debating whether he should take the next step.

'Go on say it,' she taunted, unable to help herself. It was happening, as she'd known from the moment he slid the diamond ring on her finger it would.

'You're not the woman I thought you were.'

They looked at each other, blinking and catching their breath and, as what he'd said sank in, Aisling wrenched the ring from her finger and slid it across the table toward him. She pushed her seat back and weaved her way blindly across the floor. She was vaguely aware of Alasdair's voice calling after her, not Quinn's, as the tears she'd held back the whole time she'd been in the bistro poured down her cheeks. She hoped for the briefest of seconds he'd come after her, contrite and offering her a way to make everything okay but the door to the restaurant remained closed. Her heart was in a vice, being squeezed so tight she could hardly breathe, as she made her way home, penning a letter to self all the way.

Dear Aisling,

I've lost the man I loved through my own stupidity. How am I supposed to get through this?

Yours faithfully,

Me.

Chapter 30

The banging on her bedroom door woke Aisling with a start. She was lying on her side in a tangle of sheets and for one blissful moment she couldn't understand why her eyes were glued together. She prised them open and it was like peering through the slats in a venetian blind. The realisation she was still in last night's clothes and the reason her eyes were so swollen was because she'd cried herself to sleep, broke over her. With a small moan she dug around in the trenches recalling how she'd swept in through reception last night, ignoring Nina to take to the stairs. She'd been desperate for the sanctity of her bedroom where she could let her tears out in peace. Poor Nina had received the rough end of the stick from Bronagh, and then later from herself. She owed her an apology.

Moira had been out and she'd locked her bedroom door before throwing herself down on her bed and sobbing into her pillow. It must have been in the small hours when she'd finally crashed out only to be woken a short while later by the familiar clatter of the rubbish bin in the courtyard below. She'd padded over to the window in time to see Mr Fox making his escape with whatever leftover treat Mrs Flaherty had tossed out. He turned, as he always did, and looked up to where she was a ghostly outline looking down at him. She waved through the frosted glass and he flicked his tail before flattening his back and disappearing under the wall.

Now the memory of what had transpired with Quinn was like a bucket of cold water being tossed over her. She was no longer engaged. She was right back where she'd been when Marcus left her. A jilted bride-to-be. The difference this time was, she only had herself to blame for the predicament she was in. It was down to her own stupidity and the realisation made her breath feel ragged as it caught in her chest. The banging started up again.

Maybe it was Quinn! The thought was a spurring jolt. He might have seen, in the cold light of day, that what she'd said last night had an element of truth to it. He had switched off when it came to their wedding. He could've come to his senses and be prepared to talk things through. It wasn't too late. They could sit down together to discuss what was frivolous and what was a necessity. Moira's voice blew out the tiny flame of hope she'd been fanning. 'Aisling, what's going on?'

'Go away, Moira.'

'Paula told Tom you gave your ring back to Quinn and walked out of the bistro last night in tears.'

She should've known it wouldn't take long for the jungle drums to begin beating. She repeated herself, 'Go away, Moira. I don't want to talk about it.'

'What was that? I can't hear you, Aisling. I need to know you're okay, open the door.'

She knew full well her sister had heard her; she was trying to trick her into opening the door.

When it didn't work, Moira changed tack. 'Aisling, if you come out, I cross my heart hope to die promise I'll waive stair-climbing today and I'll personally go downstairs to ask Mrs Flaherty to whip you up one of her specials and not say a word to Bronagh about you breaking your diet.'

Aisling didn't answer. She'd be sick if she tried to eat and what was the point in dieting and doing the stairs anyway? No point whatsoever now she was no longer getting married. She rolled over on her back and, as she stared up at the ceiling, she felt dead inside.

'I'll ring Mammy and tell her you won't come out of your room.'

'Do your worst, Moira,' Aisling threw back.

No reply was forthcoming and Aisling shut her eyes, hoping she could sleep forever like Aurora from *Sleeping Beauty*. It was an ironic thought given she was guessing she was anything but a beauty at the moment. She closed her eyes again but they flicked open of their own accord as she examined what had happened between her and Quinn. In the half light of her bedroom it was becoming clear to her she'd pushed away the person who meant the most to her in the whole world because she hadn't felt deserving of him. In a roundabout way Marcus McDonagh had reached out from her past, refusing to let her move on and accept Quinn's love wholeheartedly. She'd subconsciously been sabotaging their relationship by behaving like an extravagant eejit. There she'd been burning up her credit card as though she were some sort of cashed-up celebrity. And what did it matter, any of it? The dress, the carriage, the place settings – in the big picture they didn't mean a thing. What her wedding should have been about was standing alongside Quinn and turning to look him in the eyes. She should have been focussing on how it would feel to see her love for him reflected back at her in his face as he told God, their family and friends he wanted to spend the rest of his life with her.

AISLING MUST HAVE DOZED off again because this time when she woke, she could sense the lateness of the morning by the way chunks of filtered light broke through the curtains. She strained her ears listening out for Moira and caught the swish of whispering. So, Moira had made good on her threat and called Mammy. She had a more pressing problem than the fact her mammy was standing outside her bedroom door pow-wowing with her baby sister as to what they should say to lure her out. Aisling knew it wouldn't be whatever pearls of wisdom they shouted through the door that brought her out. It would be the fact she was desperate for the loo. The days of the chamber pot were long gone unfortunately and she was going to have to visit the bathroom, like it or not.

She sat up, vaguely aware her eyes were still hot and heavy. Her hand smoothed her hair but it had matted itself into a frenzy of knots, thanks to her tossing and turning. It would take more than running her fingers through it. She swung her legs over the side of the bed and stood up, surprised to feel the floor firm beneath her feet. She'd almost thought she might fall through it like Alice going down the rabbit hole because that was how she felt, as if she'd fallen through into some strange world she no longer recognised.

She moved toward the door and flung it open, stepping back as Mammy and Moira staggered forward nearly falling on top of her. 'That will teach you for pressing your ears to my door. Now, get out of my way because I need to go to the loo.' Aisling pushed past them and through to the lavatory, locking yet another door behind her. She rested her head against it for a moment and then yelled out, 'And don't stand outside the door. That always gives me stage fright. I'll talk to you when I come out.'

She heard a gratifying creak as they moved away. It was with trepidation she opened the door after flushing but the coast was clear and she slipped into the bathroom next door. A hot shower and a change of clothes was in order if she had to deal with Mammy and she knew without looking, she and Moira would have taken up camp on the sofa and neither would be leaving until they'd got to the bottom of what had gone on between her and Quinn.

A STEAMING MUG OF SWEETENED tea was placed on the table in front of her along with a plate of thickly buttered toast. Aisling stared at it, watching the golden puddles pool and melt into the toast.

'You're no good on an empty stomach, Aisling.' Maureen fussed around her. 'You've never been able to make rational decisions when you're hungry. Personally, I'm pointing the finger for all this bother at...' She flapped her hand in Moira's direction.

Moira dropped the piece of toast she'd been chewing on down on the plate and straightened from where she'd been slouched over the kitchen worktop. 'That's not fair, Mammy. I was trying to help. Aisling was the one who wanted to lose a few pounds for the wedding.'

'Don't talk with your mouth full. And did she want the spotty, red face too? Look at her, I mean look at her. People will be giving her a wide berth thinking she's contagious. What were you thinking?'

The hives were clinging on stubbornly. Aisling was blaming stress but there was no need for Mammy to point them out quite so emphatically. It wasn't the spots that had caused all this trouble.

'I didn't know she'd react to the pack I used,' Moira pouted.

'You know full well your sister has always had sensitive skin, young lady. Sure, she spent half her childhood slathered in the E45 because of some rash or other.'

Aisling didn't have the energy to protest this exaggeration. From memory she'd only had a nasty rash once. It was from eating too many strawberries. There was no point mentioning this to Mammy though. She'd twist the story around so instead of being a greedy girl with a penchant for strawberries it would morph into Aisling's first foray into stress eating. She'd blame it on the falling out she and Leila had had. The falling out part was true; they'd had a stand-off over who was the best looking member of Duran Duran. She was with John and Leila was backing Simon and ne'er the twain do meet. The point of this silent debate she was having was, the only reason she got a rash from strawberries was because she ate too many of the fecking things.

'Be quiet the pair of you.' She slapped the table to distract herself as much as Mammy and Moira. They blinked at her and then both spoke over the top of one another. 'Tom said Paula said you threw your ring back at Quinn.' 'Moira's after telling me you've called the wedding off.'

Aisling shook her head. 'Do you want to know what happened?' It was a stupid question and her answer lay in their frenetic nodding.

She took a gulp of her milky tea and then began to talk, 'Quinn wanted us to buy a house on the Crumlin Road as a rental investment. We'd been to the bank and had a verbal agreement with the manager as to what sum we could borrow based on the deposit we had.'

'Very sensible young man, your Quinn, one in a million so he is,' Mammy said.

'He's not my Quinn, Mammy. Not any more, because I'm not sensible I'm a fecking eejit.'

Maureen didn't have the heart to tell her to watch her mouth.

'I spent the best part of the deposit on the wedding without telling him.'

'So, it's your fault.'

'Moira that's not helpful,' Maureen snapped. 'But Aisling what about what I offered to put towards the wedding.'

Moira's gaze whiplashed toward her mammy. 'You never said you were giving Aisling money, and me a poor student.'

Maureen gave her youngest child a look that could curdle milk straight from the cow and Moira busied herself with her toast.

Aisling shrugged. 'It's all gotten out of hand, Mammy. The dress, the bridesmaids' dresses, the photographer, the pumpkin carriage—'

'The pumpkin what?' Moira snorted. 'Who do you think you are, Cinderella?'

Aisling swung around in her seat, her temper fraying. 'And you didn't help with your poor student routine. Do you have any idea how much those dresses cost? Did you even look at the price tag?' Her voice was shrill.

'Don't blame me,' Moira shouted back. 'You offered.'

Aisling drew breath but Maureen intervened. 'Moira O'Mara, go to your room right now and don't come out until you've something helpful to say,' Maureen ordered.

'Mammy, I'm twenty-five. You can't send me to my room.'

'You're still my daughter and not too old to feel the back of my hand.' Maureen stared her daughter down – the Mammy Whisperer – Moira slunk off to her bedroom.

'I don't know where we got that one from.' She shook her head watching her go. She let Aisling drain her tea before leaning across the table and smoothing a wisp of hair stuck to her daughter's cheek. 'Well, my girl, what are we going to do to fix this? Your Uncle Cormac is somewhere over the Atlantic about now. Great Aunty Noreen telephoned to say she and Great Aunty Rosamunde are riding up together, not to mention the Brothers Grimm will be dusting off their suits about now.'

Aisling bit back the smile that came unbidden at her mammy's referencing of her brothers.

'I don't know how to fix it though, Mammy. What do I do?'

'Aisling, you are a marvel at sorting other people's lives out but when it comes to your own,' she shook her head. 'Talk to him,' she offered up simply. 'If you can't talk to each other then you shouldn't be getting married. Your daddy and I had an unspoken rule in our marriage.'

Aisling looked up meeting her mammy's dark eyes. 'What was it?'

'We'd never go to sleep on an argument.'

Aisling sparked at the blatant fib. 'Mammy, that's not true! I remember you giving Daddy the silent treatment for nearly a week when we were small.'

'Ah, well now, Aisling, that was different. Your daddy had been very bold.'

Aisling's scalp prickled. She never had found out what the week was about where Mammy had communicated through Roisin, 'Tell your daddy, I said he can cook his own tea tonight.'. Had he been unfaithful? 'What did he do, Mammy?' she half whispered, fearful of finding out.

'He spent the money I'd set aside for a new dress to wear to my friend Geraldine's birthday party on an engine overhaul for the car.'

Aisling nearly laughed with the relief of it all.

'What I was trying to say, Aisling, before you started nit-picking was, a marriage needs three simple ingredients to thrive. I like to call it the three 'c's'

'What are they?'

'Communication and compromise.'

'That's only two.'

'I can't remember the third, it might have been compassion or care for one another. I told you to stop picking holes. You get the idea.'

'Well Quinn and I aren't doing very well are we, Mammy? We haven't even gotten to the church and we can't find a way to compromise.'

'Ah, but you will, Aisling, because you and Quinn are like me and your daddy. You're meant to be together.'

A voice bellowed, 'Can I come out now?!'

Aisling and Maureen looked at one another and exchanged complicit smiles. 'No, you can't!'

Chapter 31

Cormac O'Mara stood in the guesthouse lobby, larger than life for a little man, his Louis Vuitton luggage abandoned on either side of him as he waited for Maureen to bring the last case in. He'd been unable to carry it all himself because he was a man who believed in packing for all occasions, except it would seem he thought, shaking off the cold, the inclement Irish weather. He was making a statement in his trademark crumpled linen suit which was highly unsuitable for flying and for the country he found himself back in. He refused to kow-tow to the norm though, or to be sensible. He'd had far too many years doing so as a younger man in Dublin and it had nearly quashed his spirit. A quick check was in order next, to ensure the infernal wind gusting down the street outside hadn't dislodged his hair. He patted the top of his head, yes, yes, all was as it should be.

The woman who'd worked here since time began and whose name he tried to conjure, Breda or Brenda, something like that was staring over at him. He bared the perfectly aligned teeth he'd spent a small fortune on in her direction.

Bronagh blinked, feeling warmed by the glow of his neon smile. Cormac was the first of the wedding guests to arrive at O'Mara's. The guesthouse was at the sole disposal of family and friends for the next four nights. It had been no mean feat to ensure the window of time had been kept clear and it had all been for nothing. Sparks were sure to fly when he learned he'd had a wasted journey she thought, frantically swiping the telltale biscuit crumbs off her lap and getting to her feet. Her calves were sore from this morning's stair climb. She'd tried to get out of it, telling Moira all bets were off until Aisling made an appearance in reception and confirmed she was still in the running. Moira was having none of it and had warned Bronagh, given Aisling's lovesick state the odds were against her. Bronagh's competitive streak had reared and bucked and she'd taken to those stairs as though she were entering into the Olympic stair climbing race. She'd earned herself a biscuit or two, she reassured herself, turning her attention to Cormac O'Mara.

She'd only met him a handful of times and each time she'd been struck by yer man's resemblance, not to his late brother, God rest his soul, but to Elton John. She'd have loved to ask him if he could give her a few lines of *Rocketman* but had never summoned the nerve. She swept out from behind her desk, her hand extended, 'Welcome home, Mr O'Mara. It's grand to see you.' The consummate professional.

'Please, call me Cormac, Brandy.' He returned her handshake briefly.

'Bronagh,' she corrected, wondering whether all those rings on his fingers had left an indentation on her palm. He smelt very nice too, for a man who'd just come off a long-haul flight, and she tried not to sniff too obviously. The scent of pine made a pleasant change from the Arpège and fried bacon. Cormac was too busy looking about the entrance of his childhood home to acknowledge his gaffe. She marvelled over him being short and well- padded where his brother had been tall and lanky. There were similarities too though in certain expressions and she wondered if Maureen felt her loss keenly all over again when she caught sight of them.

The door opened once more and the woman herself, windswept and hobbling like Quasi Modo, appeared with the last of Cormac's designer bags. Pooh pranced in alongside her, all sugar and spice and all things nice. Bronagh eyeballed the poodle, she had the measure of him right enough. He was not to be trusted.

'Jaysus wept,' Maureen muttered, dropping the bag down next to the others. 'Are you after moving back to Dublin, Cormac?'

'Not a chance, Mo. LA is the land of sunshine. It's been good to me whereas Ireland is the land of—'

'Rainbows,' Maureen stated firmly.

Bronagh raised an eyebrow. Mo indeed.

Cormac had not been about to say the country where he'd grown up was the land of rainbows but he swallowed his words. There was nothing to be gained by allowing his acerbic tongue to get the better of him and besides he was fond of Mo, a name he'd called her from the get-go. It was for this reason he'd decided to behave himself and as such he changed the subject. 'The old place is looking good. I hope you'll be giving me the grand tour.'

'Of course I will, and this,' Maureen arced her hand in a sweeping movement, 'could have all been yours, Cormac, if you hadn't of been so desperate to get on the boat and leave us all behind.'

Bronagh's eyes widened at the thought of this flamboyant man at the helm of the guesthouse. She wondered if he knew Elton – he did live in Los Angeles after all. Sure, they were always rubbing shoulders with the rich and famous out there. Patrick was after telling her he knew yer man, Cruise. They frequented the same juice bar. She wondered if Patrick, Cindy and Cormac all went to the same dentist.

'A decision that worked out well for us all.'

'That it did.'

They smiled at each other and Pooh nuzzled up next to this new member of his family.

'He likes you.' Maureen was pleased. Cormac hadn't made a fuss like Roisin over sitting in the back of the car when she'd picked him up from the airport. He said he was used to it. Apparently, he had a driver over there in Los Angeles.

'Where's the bride-to-be? I thought she'd be here to greet me, given you've officially handed over the baton, Mo.' Cormac pouted. He was a little put out. He'd come a long way after all and the least his middle niece could do was be here when he arrived.

'Erm, Aisling's upstairs. Moira's at college and said to tell you she's looking forward to seeing you.' She pursed her lips knowing full well Moira was hoping her fashion-king uncle had brought gifts from the Land of Plenty with him. 'Patrick and Cindy are due in the day before the erm, ah, the erm wedding because Cindy had a bra commercial to film and Roisin's arriving from London with young Noah tomorrow.' She'd filled Roisin in on the unfolding drama of Aisling and Quinn but had told her she should still come because it wasn't over until the fat lady sings. Roisin had shaken her head, and told her mammy that she wasn't fat, cuddly yes, but not fat. Maureen had been put out and had huffed she hadn't been speaking literally. 'Noah's a dote so he is,' she told Cormac, her arms already itching with the urge to wrap him in a big hug. 'Now then, Cormac, let's get you settled in your room and then we'll go upstairs and have ourselves a nice cup of tea and catch up.'

'Green tea?' Cormac asked hopefully.

'Sure, tea's tan not green and anything else isn't tea, you eejit,' Maureen tutted before telling him she'd find their housekeeper, Ita, and get her to give them a hand with his luggage. She was eager to get Cormac away from the reception area. He was prone to dramatics and she had a feeling they were in for an explosion when he learned Aisling had announced the wedding was not going ahead despite her best efforts to talk sense into her daughter yesterday. The way things currently stood, he'd had a wasted journey.

For his part, Cormac may not have seen his sister-in-law for a good while but she had a face he could read like a book and he raised an eyebrow.

It was a lovely shape so it was, Bronagh thought, looking on and smoothing her own pencil thin ones. His skin had a glowing sheen to it too, she noticed. She could do with more glow; she'd have to ask him what products he was after using.

'Is there something I should know, Mo?'

Maureen ignored him. 'Pooh, you stay there with your uncle Cormac.' She took to the stairs calling out Ita's name.

Bronagh began whistling *Rocketman* and looking everywhere but at Cormac.

Chapter 33

Maureen found Ita looking shifty in Room 3, and enlisted her to help them haul Cormac's luggage to his room. The housekeeper obliged with far more grace than she would have Aisling, but then it wasn't Aisling who was friendly with her mammy and liable to tell tales. She'd have liked to have had a few moments to admire the strange little man with the mat on top of his head's Vuitton cases because one day she'd travel the world with expensive luggage but for now she did as she was asked and followed Maureen's lead dragging the case up the stairs to Room 5.

Maureen had personally done a sweep of Cormac's room before she'd left to collect him. It was important to her that he saw first-hand what a success she and Brian had made of the guesthouse, even after all these years. Room 5 with its old-world elegance was a nod to the Georgian grandeur of the building. It afforded a grand view over the Green and as such it was one of her favourites. The pillows had been plumped by her personally, the bathroom inspected, and the bed smoothed. Her reward for her efforts came when Cormac made appreciative murmurs as he inspected his quarters. 'It's hardly recognisable from the days when Mammy and Dad ran the place.'

'It was different times and they did a grand job. We just brought it up to date,' Maureen said loyally; she'd been fond of Brian's parents. They'd been good to her and the bitter feelings between Mr and Mrs O'Mara senior and Cormac had been nothing to do with her. Like she'd said, it was different times. Cormac had been long gone when she'd come door knocking to the guesthouse seeking work, never dreaming she'd marry the handsome young man who'd opened the door to her and that one day they'd run the place. Brian hadn't spoken of his older brother often. On those few occasions when Cormac had come back to Ireland it had been clear to her why he'd gone. It was a truth the family had refused to acknowledge and in doing so had ensured he could never be at home in his own country. It saddened Maureen to think he'd shared his home with his partner Ricardo for over twenty years but even now wasn't comfortable bringing the person he'd chosen to spend his life with here to Ireland to meet them.

On the bright side her brother-in-law was a particular so and so but he was happy with the room she'd chosen for him and that was high praise. She was pleased because, once she got him away from Ita's flapping ears and up to the privacy of the family apartment to explain what was going on with her daughter, he was going to be anything but happy. A sudden movement caught her eye. 'Don't even think about it, Pooh,' she warned the poodle, who was inching toward the bed having decided it was as good a place as any for a siesta. Pooh froze and gave her what she recognised as his affronted look. The 'as if I would do something like that' expression. Ita was still loitering in the doorway. 'Thanks for your help.' She dismissed her with a smile but she wasn't quick enough to stop Cormac from whipping out his wallet.

He handed a wad of notes to Ita who looked like the cat who'd got the cream. The American guests were her favourite and thanking him, she stuffed the money in the pocket of her smock before taking herself off. She could sense Maureen's disapproval of her taking the tip from him given he was family. Well, tough, she'd interrupted her in the middle of a game of Snake and her phone was burning a hole in her pocket. It was high time she got back to it.

'Come on then, Cormac, let's get you upstairs,' Maureen said, giving him the card he'd need to access his room. She shooed Pooh out of the door ahead of her and headed up the last flight of stairs.

Cormac dawdled up behind her, muttering about elevators having been invented for over a hundred years. The apartment was, again, vastly different from his childhood memories where everything had seemed tired and worn out like the building itself. Maureen had a flair when it came to interiors. He liked the ambience she'd created. What he didn't like was the growing sensation that all was not as it should be. Maureen had begun to act skittish as she moved about the kitchen fetching cups and saucers and there was still no sign of Aisling.

'Mo, I have swapped the beautiful sunshine and palm trees of LA for winter in Dublin. Please tell me the wedding is going ahead this Saturday.'

If he'd been hoping she'd be taken aback by the intimation anything was wrong then he'd have been disappointed. He watched as her mouth performed a dance of indecision before she called out, 'Aisling O'Mara, get out here now and explain to your uncle Cormac, who's flown all the way from Los Angeles what's going on.'

It took a moment or two but Aisling mooched forth looking like she'd been sleeping rough and Cormac gave her a head to toe once over before stamping his Versace clad foot. 'No, absolutely not, Aisling. Not a second time. I'm not having it.'

Aisling stared at him dully, she'd have thought Mammy would have told everybody not to come. She was the one in charge of the guest list. She tried to catch her eye but Maureen was feigning great interest in the tea she was brewing.

'You are not cancelling on me twice, Aisling. Now, sit yourself down and tell me what's happened.'

It was a funny thing, Aisling thought, doing as she was told, but when her uncle was mad his American accent became decidedly Irish. Cormac sat down next to her, kicking off his loafers, and she tried not to fixate on his sock clad feet as he began rotating his fat ankles in little circles. He looked at her in a way that brooked no nonsense and she caught a glimpse of her daddy in his features. It made her feel warm inside and she found herself babbling the whole sorry story out. Maureen brought his tea over, making unhelpful mmm noises at different points in Aisling's monologue.

When Aisling had run dry, Cormac looked at her. 'Is that all? You've quibbled over a few pounds?'

'It was more than a few pounds, Uncle Cormac.'

'Pfft.' He made a motion with his hand as though it were a matter too trivial to be bothered with. 'Well, you don't need to worry because your fairy godmother is here now. Once I've had my tea and my ankles have returned to their normal size, we are off to see that fiancé of yours.'

Maureen gave a strangled cough as her tea went down the wrong way.

Chapter 34

Quinn and Aisling were seated opposite each other at the table in the kitchen of his mammy and daddy's house. They were both studying the rings left behind by hot drinks over the years, the marks of family life. The sweet smell of baking hung on the air but there was no cosiness to be found in the sugary smells. Aisling had her hands folded in her lap and Cormac was sitting at the head of the table like a presiding judge. She felt as if she'd been called to the headmistress's office for a playground misdemeanour. If only she could get a rap over the knuckles and be done with it but Quinn hadn't looked at her, not once, since Cormac had ordered them both to sit down. She felt sick and wasn't even the slightest bit tempted to help herself to one of Mrs Moran's brownie biscuits. There was no way she could call her Maeve, not now. Unlike her mammy who'd been all, 'Now then, Maeve, what are we going to do about these children of ours?' And whom she suspected right now had her head together with Quinn's mammy in the living room discussing their eejitty children.

If Mrs Moran had been surprised to find a washed-out Aisling, Maureen O'Mara, and a little man in a *Miami Vice* suit and a hair piece standing on her doorstep that damp Dublin afternoon, she'd hidden it well. She'd been gracious, ushering them in out of the cold before fussing about making tea. She'd even managed to retrieve a herbal teabag for Cormac. There was no need for him to know it had been lurking down the back of her cupboard since Ivo had gone out with that girl with the dippy hippy ways a few years back. If anything, Maeve was grateful that someone was taking matters in hand and she had a feeling that Cormac was the right man for the job.

Quinn had not come quietly, protesting all the way from his room, but he'd clammed up when he saw the trio of O'Maras standing around the kitchen table. He'd managed to shake Cormac's hand and mumble hellos to Maureen and Aisling. He was well mannered her boy, even if he was an eejit. He hadn't looked Aisling in the eye but she'd seen Aisling risk a glance from under her lashes at him. Her mouth had parted a little, startled by his dishevelled appearance. Maeve had tried to talk sense into her son by telling him Aisling had gotten carried away, that was all, but he was cut from the same cloth as his father and it was a stubborn one. She'd even had to remind him to shower like she'd had to when he was a teenager these last few days. She gave a surreptitious sniff hoping he'd remembered to put deodorant on.

She'd hovered on the edge of the group unsure how this would go but when Cormac asked the young couple to sit down so they could have a chat, his manner had them both doing as they were told. He was a little like a male Judge Judy she'd thought, linking her arm through Maureen's, assured things were going to be just fine. She suggested they take their tea and enjoy a slice of brownie in the front room. It would be nice to get to know Aisling's mammy a little better.

'Right then,' Cormac said, and if he'd had a gavel, Aisling suspected he would have banged it down. Instead he had to make do with placing his mug on the table. 'Aisling, I want you to explain to Quinn why you behaved like a mad woman over this wedding.'

Aisling grasped her hands a little tighter and licked her lips. She had nothing to lose by opening up. 'It doesn't make much sense, Quinn, but from the minute you put my beautiful ring on my finger I had this sinking feeling something would go wrong. I suppose I felt that because Marcus called everything off, I wasn't worthy of being married and so to compensate I overcompensated by trying to bury those thoughts in buying and booking things.'

'Bling, darling,' Cormac elaborated for her before turning to Quinn. 'You don't have to be a psychiatrist to work out that her compulsive spending was a reaction to the anxiety she was feeling. I've seen it time and time again on Rodeo Drive where my boutique is. Women throwing the cash around to try to make their problems go away.'

Quinn nodded. He got it, he did, but what he didn't get was why she hadn't trusted him. He put voice to this.

Aisling dug her nails into her palms and her voice was tinny. 'I do trust you. It's me I didn't trust.'

Quinn looked bewildered but didn't get a chance to probe further because Cormac was pointing at him. 'You're on.'

'Um,' Quinn hesitated.

'Come on, you're a chef, you should be good at expressing your feelings.'

He found the right words. 'I never wanted a big wedding, Aisling, but I didn't want to upset you because you were a force to be reckoned with. You'd ask my opinion but I could see you didn't want it, you wanted me to agree with whatever you were suggesting. All I wanted was to say our vows, me and you in front of our family and friends. Then celebrate with a party at the restaurant. Simple.' He gave a shrug as though he still couldn't believe how hard it had all gotten.

There was truth in his words. Aisling knew it had been her way or the highway. Her face felt hot and not because of the spots, they'd finally disappeared, but because she'd been so unfair. 'I'm sorry, Quinn.'

Cormac looked at Aisling and then at Quinn. They both looked to him wondering what he'd say next. 'Do you love, Aisling, Quinn?'

'Of course, I do.'

Aisling's eyes welled and a plump tear formed on her lower lashes.

Cormac nodded – this was going exactly how he'd planned. 'And, Aisling, do you love Quinn?'

'More than anything.' The tear rolled down her cheek.

'Do you remember the Beatles?' Cormac asked.

This was getting weird, Quinn thought. 'Yeah, who doesn't?'

Aisling agreed with his sentiment.

'Well as Paul sang, all you need is love.'

Aisling and Quinn locked eyes. It was Quinn who spoke first. 'Shall we start again?'

'I'd like that.'

Quinn reached over and brushed the tear from Aisling's cheek. Cormac cleared his throat and got up from his seat. Humming the classic Beatles tune, he decided his work was done. It was time to leave them to it and he wouldn't mind another slice of that brownie either.

Chapter 35

Noreen's case lay open on her bed and she folded the last of the necessities she'd need for her stay in Dublin, placing them carefully around the vase she'd bought for Aisling and Quinn. It was well padded and she'd be sure to tell Terry not to be throwing her case around when he put it in the boot. He and Rosamunde would be here shortly to pick her up. She'd hang her outfit from the handle about the window in the back of the car. She checked her watch again wishing the hands would turn faster. It was still a good twenty minutes until they were due to collect her and she was unable to settle, thanks to the nervous excitement about what lay in store these next few days. Emer, she'd gleaned from Rosamunde, was living an hour out of Dublin and planned on meeting her mammy, daddy, and the rest of her siblings, who were also spread far and wide these days, at the church. Sadly, her marriage had broken down this last year and as such she'd be attending on her own. She wasn't bringing her children either who were nearly adults now and had no interest in attending the wedding of a sort of cousin they barely knew.

The thought of Emer's children nearly grown up was a reminder of the lost years and Noreen pushed those rogue thoughts away. The past couldn't be changed; it was what lay ahead that mattered.

Chapter 35
The day of the wedding

U ncle Cormac was indeed her fairy godmother, Aisling thought, admiring the way the tiny crystals on the bodice of her dress sparkled under the light. She felt like a princess. He'd insisted on footing the bill for hers and her bridesmaids' dresses. 'Aisling,' he'd said bossily, 'I have dedicated my life to fashion and a girl should have the dress of her dreams on her wedding day but a pumpkin carriage,' he'd shaken his head, 'she does not need.'

'You've got my something borrowed?' Roisin checked, and Aisling dutifully lifted the heavy fabric of her gown to display the garter belt her eldest sister had worn at her own wedding. Roisin grinned, 'I hope it brings you the sort of wedding night I had.'

Aisling wrinkled her nose at the thought of Colin and Rosi doing the deed. She knew they had to have done so at least once or they wouldn't have had Noah but still she preferred to think her nephew had been an immaculate conception.

'He was many things, my ex-husband—' Roisin continued.

'A chinless feck for one,' Moira piped up.

Roisin ignored her, 'But in those early days believe it or not, he was quite the ride.'

There was a collective gagging sound from Moira and Aisling.

'What are you on about?' Mammy bustled over. She'd been practising her mysterious mammy-of-the-bride look as she peered out from under the hat sitting heavy on her head thanks to the weight of all those feathers. If she were to venture into rural Ireland she'd be in danger of being pecked at by hens, Moira had said upon seeing it.

Feathers aside, Aisling thought, giving her mammy the once-over, she did look beautiful and she had a spring in her step of late that made Aisling wonder about this man friend of hers. When she got back from her honeymoon, she'd sit down with her and make her talk. The offer of tea and a bun at Bewley's should do the trick. Adrenalin ricocheted through her. She'd be a married woman by then, she'd be Mrs Aisling O'Mara-Moran sitting down having a very adult conversation about relationships with her mammy.

'I've given her the something blue,' Moira chirped up.

Aisling had been touched that, despite her sister's constant referencing of her student poverty, she'd splashed out what funds she had on a pearl studded, pale blue hair slide, fixing it in her sister's hair herself. She'd stood back admiring her hand-iwork. Aisling had decided not to ask her if she'd splurged her bookkeeping earnings to buy the barrette. The odds had been on her winning the great weight loss race and she hadn't disappointed. Moira, as such, was in the money. Bronagh's sulk had only lasted a day, by the end of which they were all sick to the back teeth of hearing how Aisling had had an unfair advantage because she wasn't suffering the ravages of the menopause.

The gift that had brought tears to her eyes along with shrieks from Moira that she was not to cry or her mascara would run, was from Maeve. It finally felt right to call Quinn's mammy by her name. She'd knocked on the door to the family apartment at the guesthouse earlier that morning having made the journey especially so she could present Aisling with a delicate gold chain with a single pearl set in a daisy filigree of white gold. 'It was my mammy's, Aisling,' she'd said. 'I wore it when I married Quinn's dad and I want you to have it now.'

Aisling knew it was her way of welcoming her into the family and she was touched. She was also relieved her hat wasn't bigger than Mammy's or there'd have been ructions.

Leila was making the rounds of the living room checking over her charges. She had been a superstar these last two days dealing with all the cancellations. With a smile of satisfaction on her face, Leila announced. 'Well, I think we have time for a glass of bubbles before Ned arrives.'

'Mummy, can I have bubbles?' Noah beseeched Roisin. He was bored of all the primping and fussing.

'No, you can't. Bubbles aren't for children.'

'Ah sure, a tiny sip won't hurt him, Roisin,' Maureen bossed. Her grandson was back in her good books after yesterday's misdemeanour. She'd been mortified when she'd introduced him to Cormac and he'd asked if he had a gerbil on top of his head. Cormac had not been amused.

Leila popped the cork and did the honours, passing out the flutes.

'Thanks for this, Leila.' Moira said, raising her sparkling grape juice.

'You're a bad influence, Mammy,' Roisin said, seeing mammy give her grandson a tiny taste.

Aisling held up her glass, clearing her throat. 'You all look so beautiful, and Noah you're very handsome. I'm so blessed to have you in my life and thanks so much for putting up with me these last few weeks.'

There was a collective murmuring and Aisling picked up on Moira saying that, yes, she had been a pain in the arse but they all loved her.

She took a sip of the golden liquid, feeling giddy with happiness as the bubbles pinged in her mouth. A few mouthfuls later, the phone rang and Roisin answered it, announcing that Ned was waiting for them downstairs. Mammy led the charge.

'Mammy, don't you be doing that that thing you're after doing with your hat, or you'll trip going down the stairs,' Roisin ordered, following behind her, a firm hold on her son's hand lest he have any thought about racing off to drag Mr Nibbles along with them. The thought of the gerbil getting loose in St Theresa's made her skin prickle.

They burst out the doors of O'Mara's to where Ned was holding the door of the limousine open for them. The blonde one had convinced him to do a cut price church run. It was a first, he thought, wondering how the mammy one was going to get in the back with that rooster on her head.

Chapter 36

'To Mr and Mrs Moran!'

Mercifully her brother-in-law had finished his long-winded speech although Aisling thought, she needed him to make a tiny correction. She tapped him on the arm before he sat down. He leaned over to listen to what she had to say before straightening and clearing his throat.

'Excuse me but that should have been to Mr Moran and Mrs O'Mara-Moran.'

'To Mr Moran and Mrs O'Mara-Moran.' Glasses were raised.

Maureen's eyes prickled at the thought of how proud Brian would have been of his middle daughter today. Cormac did you proud in more ways than one she told him silently, reaching for Cormac's hand under the table and giving it a squeeze. He returned it. She blinked those rogue tears away. Today was a happy day and as such she turned her attention instead to the bistro. There were no fancy table arrangements, although they had followed her seating plan. Dinner had been the house speciality here at Quinn's, bangers 'n' mash. Paula was doing a superb job of keeping the wine flowing she saw, watching the girl scurry from table to table. Too much of a good job given how some were imbibing – her heathen brothers for starters. She gave Frankie and Brendan a hard stare and they put their glasses down. Her other brother, Colm, was in danger of a frozen neck. He hadn't moved from his position, inches away from

Cindy's cleavage, for fear of missing something, since he'd sat down. She'd have words with him later if Patrick didn't sort him out before then. Her son was glowering at his uncle. At least Roisin, Moira and Leila would be happy. Cindy's bosoms had taken the onus off them.

There was no compère. but Shay and his band were going to play shortly and were setting up on the stage now. It had all gone very well, she thought, sitting back in her chair feeling satisfied with how the day had panned out. She heard Aisling's laughter pealing across the room and she looked across at her radiant daughter. There was no doubt she was having the best day of her life. Quinn was no longer at her side and she assumed he'd gone to mingle. A finer son-in-law she couldn't have wished for and Maureen knew if she'd been given the chance to handpick the man Aisling would marry it would be him. Brian would have too.

A foreign beat flared up making her and most of the other guests jump. She saw Aisling's eyes widen, her hand fly to her mouth. Maureen swivelled her head to follow Aisling's gaze to the area in front of the stage. Holy mother of Jaysus, there was Quinn spotlighted doing some fancy footwork as he quick-stepped across the floor to the cha-cha-cha rhythm his face a study of concentration. He paused to gesture for Aisling to join him and Maureen held her breath, not knowing how she'd manage to do whatever it was she was about to do on the dance floor weighted down by that dress of hers.

Aisling didn't know either but she knew she'd do her best because it didn't matter one iota if she cocked up. She had Quinn and that was all that mattered.

NOREEN AND EMER WERE sitting next to each other, relaxed and content in each other's company as the evening moved away from dinner and into the dancing. The table in front of them had long since been cleared, leaving a cluster of drinks – some full, some dregs. She was thin, Noreen thought, soaking up the sight of her niece in her turquoise dress as she sat engrossed in the band. She'd a pinched look about her that time and an unhappy marriage had wrought. No doubt she'd found her aunt much changed too, she mused. Despite the obvious etchings of age, she'd always see that little girl so eager to help her and Malachy in the shop when she looked at her though.

Emer felt her gaze on her and turned slightly in her chair. She smiled at her aunt and took her hand in hers giving it a squeeze. Noreen squeezed back. A burden had been lifted from her shoulders tonight. Weddings were about new beginnings and the loneliness she'd felt since Malachy's passing had eased at the knowledge their niece was back in her life.

'Shall we have a dance, Aunty Nono?'

Noreen was quite sure she'd be able to dance the night away so light did she feel. 'In a minute, Emer. I promised Cormac the first dance.'

Emer gave her another smile and turned her attention back to the band, her toes tapping to the Irish beat. She too felt light, and freer than she had in a good long while. Life hadn't been kind to her since her husband had left and as for their children, well, they were selfish mares the lot of them. All too caught up in their own lives to spare a thought for their poor mammy, left on her own struggling to make ends meet. She'd be alright now though. Aunty Nono had a tidy nest egg, and sure she was entitled to a generous helping of it, who else would she leave it to?

The End

Hi! I hope this latest instalment in The Guesthouse on the Green series made you smile, or even better laugh out loud. If you enjoyed Aisling's journey to the aisle then leaving a short review on Amazon to say so would be wonderful and so appreciated. You can keep up to date with news regarding this series via my newsletter (I promise not to bombard you!) by subscribing via her website at www.michellevernalbooks.com

To say thanks, you receive an exclusive O'Mara women character profile.

Book 7, The Guesthouse on the Green Series

Maureen's Song

Out Now available through Amazon

Sometimes life is like a country and western song...

Maureen O'Mara's had a lot of changes these last few years. She lost her beloved husband, Brian, had a fresh start by the seaside away from the family guesthouse and took up numerous new hobbies, the most recent being line dancing. She's ready to make one more big change too because she's met a man. Not just any man either. A man who makes her smile, has her humming country music tunes and tapping her toes to the beat. He's also someone who understands the pain of losing a spouse.

Maureen would like to keep things as they are but he's making noises about introducing her to his family and she can't put him off forever. He wants to meet her girls too but what happens when your children have their late parent on a pedestal? And what will the O'Mara girls have to say when they find out about their mammy's new manfriend's interesting erm, hobby?

Find out in Maureen's Song.

Printed in Great Britain
by Amazon

55002847R00151